PRAISE FOR
HELEN HARDT

"Hardt delivers a brand-new series with rugged cowboys and scintillating sex. Talon and Jade's instant chemistry heats up the pages..."

~ RT Book Reviews

"Proving the masterful writer she is, Ms. Hardt continues to weave her beautifully constructed web of deceit, terror, disappointment, passion, love, and hope as if there was never a pause between releases. A true artist never reveals their secrets, and Ms. Hardt is definitely a true artist."

Bare Naked Words

"The love story between Talon and Jade continues in Obsession. An apt title to be sure, because everyone is obsessed Dear Ms. Helen Hardt, I toss many profanities your way for making me wait. Though I give you my deepest gratitude for building the anticipation of what I'm sure will be an epic culmination to an amazing series. "

~ Heroes and Heartbreakers

Possession

STEEL BROTHERS SAGA
BOOK THREE

Possession

STEEL BROTHERS SAGA
BOOK THREE

WATERHOUSE PRESS

DEDICATION

For my two amazing, handsome, and talented sons,
Eric and Grant.

May you find happiness in every moment.

WARNING

This book contains adult language and scenes, including flashbacks of child physical and sexual abuse, which may cause trigger reactions. This story is meant only for adults as defined by the laws of the country where you made your purchase. Store your books and e-books carefully where they cannot be accessed by younger readers.

PROLOGUE

Jade

"Hello, Wendy," I said into the receiver. "This is Jade Roberts again from Snow Creek."

A heavy sigh whooshed through the phone line and into my ears. "What can I do for you, Jade?"

"You can tell me about the relationship between Larry Wade and Daphne Steel."

Silence for a few moments. Then, "I don't know what you're talking about."

"I have reason to believe that Larry Wade and Daphne Steel were half-brother and half-sister."

And again, silence.

"Look, Wendy, I know you don't want to get involved in this, but I care about the Steels."

"You're just doing Larry's dirty work."

"Yes, and no. I'm researching them for him for classified reasons, but as you know, I have my own agenda."

More silence.

"Why did someone tamper with Daphne's birth certificate and marriage certificate? Why didn't anyone think to change her father's first and middle names while they were in there?"

"I'm not sure what tree you're barking up, Jade, but I don't know what you're talking about."

"Look, I'm not stupid. The last name on Daphne's marriage certificate is Wade. Her birth certificate notes that her father's name is Jonathan Conrad Warren. Larry Wade's father is Jonathan Conrad Wade."

Another heavy sigh. "Well, you're the attorney," she said. "Piece together the evidence."

"I already have pieced it together. What I want to know is *why*."

"I'm afraid I can't tell you that."

"Why not?"

"Because I'm not sure I know myself."

I didn't believe her, of course. In my mind's eye, I saw her stroking her cheek with her index finger. But I wasn't ready to pack up everything and fly out to talk to her again if she wasn't willing to cooperate.

"All right, Wendy. I understand. If you ever feel differently about things, please call me. You have my number."

We said our goodbyes and ended the call.

I shifted my focus to a couple of DUIs for the remainder of the day. I was due in court in the morning for arraignments. Besides, I had to let go of the Steels for a few hours. As much as I loved Talon and the rest of his family, I needed to escape it all, if only for a few hours. This research was taking its toll.

When I finished work on the DUIs, I got on the Internet to look at tattoo shops in Grand Junction. Maybe I'd drive into the city over the weekend and check one of them out. Maybe find a new image. One that wouldn't upset Talon so much.

I was sipping from a bottle of water when Larry stuck his head inside my office.

"I'm taking off early, Jade," he said. "Did you need anything before I go?"

I pushed some documents across my desk. "Just your signature on these."

"Sure, no problem." He entered my office, clad in shorts, a Hawaiian-print shirt, flip-flops.

"Going to the beach?" I smiled.

"I wish. Nope, just taking the grandkids out for the afternoon. Do you have any plans for the weekend?"

"I might go into the city."

"Yeah, what for?"

"I'm thinking about getting a tattoo." My phone buzzed. "Excuse me for a minute." I picked up the receiver. "Yes?"

"It's a Ted Morse for you, Jade," Michelle said.

Colin's father? Why would he be calling me? "Okay, put him through." I turned to Larry. "I'll just be a minute."

He nodded, took the documents, and sat down in the chair opposite me, perusing them.

"This is Jade," I said into the phone.

"Jade, Ted Morse. I need some answers."

Would I ever be free of this family? "What do you mean?"

"Where the hell is my son, Jade? He was supposed to fly home after that court appearance. No one's seen him since he left here."

My blood froze in my veins. "He didn't show up in court. The last time I saw him was Saturday evening."

Silence for a few seconds, and then, "I'll be in touch." The line went dead.

Where was Colin? Dread crawled up my spine and lodged in the fine hairs on the back of my neck.

Larry sat across from me, staring. "Everything okay?"

"Yes, yes. That was my ex-fiancé's father, just looking for him."

"I see." Larry scribbled his signature on the last document. "So your tattoo. May I ask where you're getting it?"

"I don't know yet. Maybe a shop in Grand Junction."

He laughed. "I mean where on your body."

"Oh. Sure. On my lower back."

"Good spot. Your first?"

I nodded.

"They hurt like hell."

"So I've heard. But I'll be fine."

He turned to leave, and my pulse raced double-time. *Don't let him go.* I needed to know things, things that only he could tell me. And now Colin had disappeared. I doubted Larry had anything to do with that, but I feared Talon might. Damn it, I wanted some answers. So I risked losing my job and my access to all the databases. I needed to start now. For my own sanity.

"Larry?"

He turned around. "Yes?"

"Before you go, I need to ask you some questions about the Steel investigation."

"Well, as I've told you, most of that's classified, but I'll help if I can."

I drew in a breath, gathering my courage. "I want to know about your sister. Daphne Steel."

His eyes grew dark, and he walked around to my side of the desk. I trembled. But what could he do? We were in a public office, and Michelle and David were right outside. I met his angry gaze and then dropped my own to the floor, berating myself for not being able to look him in the eye.

Cheap flip-flops. But something was off.

Larry was missing a toe—the little toe on his left foot.

CHAPTER ONE

Jade

"*What* did you just say to me?" Larry's voice was dark with anger.

I lifted my gaze from his feet and looked straight into his fierce blue eyes. "I said I want to know about Daphne Steel."

"Are you sure that's all you said?"

My heart hammered wildly. Could he sense my nerves? Looking at him—his frozen blue eyes, his mouth a straight line, his creepy balding head, anger strained around his edges—I saw him for what he was.

Larry Wade was a sociopath. And I feared I had just crossed a line into dangerous territory.

I gulped and nodded. I berated myself for fearing this unethical piece of shit. But he was so close to me. The irate cold drifted from his body, frosting the air between us. Even though David and Michelle were right outside the office, I couldn't go forward with my questioning about their probable familial relationship. That would take bravery I didn't possess at the moment. So I decided to play it down, ask again without the "sister" reference, and relate it to the mysterious five-million-dollar withdrawal.

"Yes, I want to know about Daphne Steel. I think it will help the investigation."

"I thought you said something else."

I cleared my throat. "No. You must have misunderstood me."

He raised one eyebrow. God, he looked sinister. For a moment I wasn't sure he was going to say anything.

Then, "Daphne Steel died almost twenty-five years ago."

I chewed on my lower lip. "I know that. That's also right around the time when that five-million-dollar transfer was made out of one of the Steels' accounts to an unknown recipient."

Larry backed away slowly, and my panic lessened, but just a bit. If I had to, I could leapfrog over my desk and run out the door. Though in my pencil skirt and high heels, it would be a feat.

"Interesting," Larry said. "I hadn't considered that angle."

I didn't believe him for a minute. I was investigating the Steels on the city's dime, but this was very personal to Larry, despite the fact that he'd said the Steels were "good people" the first time we'd met. Why would someone want to cover up the fact that he and Daphne Steel were half-brother and half-sister? Of course, I could certainly understand why the Steels wouldn't want to be associated with him. He was a true sleazebag. Ethics meant nothing to him, and now his coldness was scaring the hell out of me.

"You told me to look for anything that was out of the ordinary. I think that's out of the ordinary."

He nodded. "It does seem odd. Have you had any luck finding out where the withdrawal went?"

I shook my head. In truth, I hadn't had the chance to investigate the withdrawal any further. I'd been too busy exploring the link between Larry and Daphne and the cover up of Talon's heroism. "They cover their tracks pretty well. I haven't been able to come up with anything."

I doubted, however, that the withdrawal had anything to do with Daphne Steel. I suspected it was related to whatever Wendy Madigan wasn't telling me about what happened twenty-five years ago.

"Honestly," Larry said, "I wouldn't go delving into Daphne Steel anymore. From what I know of her, she was very troubled. Investigating a dead woman won't lead to any pertinent information."

Maybe not for him. Besides, he hadn't shared with me the reason why he was investigating the Steels, other than his idea that they were allegedly involved in organized crime and laundering funds. I didn't believe that, not for a minute. Then again, I knew very little about Talon's father. Maybe Bradford was the place to start. Clearly, Larry didn't want me uncovering anything else with regard to Daphne.

I'd continue to do his dirty work because it meant I could help Talon, Marj, and their brothers in the process. I'd also keep my ears and eyes open for another job. I wasn't going to work for this asshole one minute longer than I had to.

I no longer felt safe here.

"Of course," I said, "if that's what you want. I won't look any further into Daphne. Enjoy your afternoon and evening with the grandkids." I hoped he'd take that as an invitation to leave.

Instead, he stared at me with his icy eyes, never blinking. Not once. I turned back to some work on my desk.

And then, "Jade?"

I looked up and met Larry's gaze. "Yes?" Invisible snakes slithered over my flesh. Just being in this close proximity with

Larry made my skin crawl. Something was off about him, and it had nothing to do with his missing toe. If my instincts were correct, it went way beyond his bending of legal ethics as well.

He curved his lips upward in a sleazy half smile. "You have a good weekend." He turned and walked slowly out of the room.

A full twenty minutes passed before I felt secure enough to stand and leave the office.

CHAPTER TWO

Talon

Dr. Carmichael was silent for a moment. Then, "I see. You weren't kidding when you said you had come through something horrific."

I cleared my throat. "No, I wasn't."

"Not that I thought you were. I figured it was something like this. Can you talk a little more about it?"

Oddly, now that I'd said the word—the word I'd kept so tightly bound within my mind for so many years—I wanted to speak. I wanted to tell her everything that had happened. And I wanted her to help me. My nerves were rattled, and my pulse raced, but I wanted—*needed*—to continue.

"Yes, I believe I can."

"All right, go on."

"They kept me locked up for over a month. Close to two, although I didn't know that at the time. The days and nights blurred together, and I had no idea how long I'd been there or what day it was when I left."

"So there were three of them?"

I nodded. "I don't remember a whole lot about them. The one who took the lead had a phoenix tattoo on his left forearm. And he had dark-brown eyes. I only remembered that recently, during the guided hypnosis."

"He seems to be the one that most of your rage is directed at."

"I've no love lost for any of them, believe me."

"Then why the focus on him? He's the one you dreamed about killing."

Why was it him? I hated all three of them to the depths of my soul. But the one with the tattoo—that mythical bird that had come to have such a contradictory meaning in my life—that one I abhorred.

I didn't know until that very moment that degrees of hate existed. But yes, I hated him most of all.

"Like I said, he was kind of the leader. Or at least that's how it seemed to me. And he had the biggest..."

God, did I really want to go there?

"Biggest what?"

I gulped. I was all in at this point. No more holding back. "He had the biggest dick. It hurt the worst when he went first."

Dr. Carmichael sat, unmoving, her lips thinning slightly. "I know this is very hard for you to talk about, Talon. So if you need to stop, just tell me. I don't have a session after yours, so we can keep going if you'd like."

What the hell? The orchard could wait. Axel was a good man. He'd take care of everything. "I don't know how long I'll be able to keep going, Doc, but I can try."

"I understand. Just tell me if you need to stop."

"All right."

Dr. Carmichael cleared her throat. "Tell me about the other two."

I closed my eyes, swallowing. "They were never as real to me as the tattoo man was. In fact, I began to think of him as Tattoo and one of the others as Low Voice. Not that his voice was abnormally low or anything. It probably wasn't even as low as mine is now. Maybe he just talked louder, but at that time, when I was ten, it seemed to me like he had a low voice."

"I see. And the third?"

"The third one was kind of in the background a lot. He was the one who always brought me food and changed the bucket where I did my business."

"Are you saying he didn't participate?"

"Oh, no. He participated. He just seemed like more of a follower than the other two, you know what I mean?"

"How did you feel about the fact that he brought you food?"

How did I feel? I had no idea where she was going. "What, you mean I was supposed to have some kind of affection for him because he fed me?"

She shook her head. "Of course not. But he *is* the one who fed you."

I closed my eyes and exhaled. "He fed me slop, Doc. It wasn't fit for pigs most of the time. But I was starving, so I ate it."

"I see."

But did she really see? She kept a noncommittal look on her face the entire time. I couldn't read her at all. Not that I was any good at reading people.

"I'm sorry you—"

I stood abruptly. "His toe."

"What do you mean?"

"I remembered something recently about the third guy, the one who brought my food. He's missing his little toe on his left foot."

"Really? So we have one guy with a phoenix tattoo on—

Which forearm?"

"The left." I sat back down and rubbed my temples.

"Okay. So he has a phoenix tattoo on his left forearm and he has brown eyes. And one of the others has a low voice, at least as you remember it, and the third is missing his little toe on his left foot, correct?"

I nodded.

"Talon, have you ever thought of trying to catch these men and bring them to justice?"

"My brothers have mentioned it from time to time. But Doc, I don't ever want to see them again. I wouldn't recognize them if they walked by me on the street anyway. They were always wearing masks. And honestly, if we did catch them. I'd just as soon dole out my own kind of justice."

"I certainly understand that feeling. But you do know that doling out your own kind of justice would land you in prison for life."

"Of course I know that. I'm not an idiot."

"I didn't mean to imply that you were. But I do know that sometimes the need for revenge can overwhelm a person."

"It doesn't really matter anyway. We'll never catch the guys. If they had any sense, they'd be long gone by now."

"Yes, they probably are."

"My older brother, Joe, he'd like to hire somebody to try to find them. I've always told him no."

"Why?"

"Because I just don't want to open it all up again."

"Isn't that what we're doing now?"

"Yes, but this is for me to heal, isn't it?"

"You're exactly right. You need to heal whether those men are caught or not. And I guess that's my point."

I sighed. "I don't think there's a chance in hell we'd ever be able to find them, Doc. They worked this area twenty-five years ago, abducted seven of us, and I was the only one to make it out alive."

"Are you positive the same men took the other children?"

Was I? I had just always assumed. "There's no way to know for sure, except for one."

"Your friend. The boy named Luke."

I nodded.

"You said he was never found."

"He wasn't. But I was the last one to see him."

"Did you see him alive?"

"No." I shook my head, my heart stampeding. "He was already dead."

"Talon, there's something I want you to understand."

"What's that?"

"None of this is your fault."

"I know that." But did I really? All those horrid days, when no one came for me, I'd sat there on that stupid raggedy blanket in that stupid gray cellar thinking I was worthless. No other reason existed for no one to come for me. "I mean, I *think* I know that."

She nodded. "What you mean is that you know that objectively. That as an adult, you know it was just chance that you were taken, and it could have easily been any other little boy in the area. You didn't deserve what happened to you any more than any of those other children did. Of course you know that. But the horror still lives inside you, and it has affected your life up until now."

That was the goddamned truth for sure.

"So even though you know it and can take a step back and

look at the situation objectively and say to yourself, 'this wasn't my fault,' it still lives inside you and affects the way you view yourself."

"I guess that's where you come in, Doc."

She smiled, and her eyes were glassy with unshed tears. "It may not be easy, but I promise you, I will not stop until we get you where we need you to be."

"Doc? I'm okay."

One tear fell down her cheek. "I know you are. And you're going to be even better."

"Then why the tears?"

"Because this is why I became a therapist, Talon. For days like today."

"What's so special about today?"

She grabbed a tissue from the box on her coffee table and wiped her eyes. "Today was the day you admitted what happened. That was the first true step in the healing process. We're not done by a long shot. It may not be pretty from here on out, but I promise you, it will at least be downhill."

CHAPTER THREE

Jade

I didn't want to be alone, but I couldn't bring myself to drive out to the ranch. It was Friday, and Marj was in the city at her cooking class. I was freaking about Larry and also about Colin being missing. I was over Colin for sure, but I didn't want anything bad to happen to him. This was a man I'd once loved, had almost spent my life with. Granted, he'd turned out to be far from the man I'd thought he was, but I still didn't wish him any ill.

Where was he?

Talon surely had nothing to do with Colin's disappearance...but I feared he might.

Talon and his brothers were good men, but even gentle and even-tempered Ryan had become rattled during their last interaction with Colin.

I desperately wanted to see Talon. Would he be home? I didn't know. Would he want to see me?

Last time we had been together, he'd told me that something unimaginable had happened to him. He was probably talking about something that had happened while he was in the Marines. But maybe...

I had told him that no matter what happened, nothing would change how I felt about him. And that was the God's honest truth.

I finished making myself a grilled cheddar-and-tomato sandwich, and I plunked down on my futon to eat it with a glass of red wine.

I had given Talon my love. I had given him my trust. I had assured him my feelings wouldn't change no matter what kind of secrets he was hiding.

What else could I do?

He had to come to me.

He was convinced he wasn't worthy of me. I couldn't begin to guess why he felt that way. What could've happened to him that was so horrible he had tried like hell to get himself killed while he was overseas? He had admitted as much to me. He didn't think of himself as a hero, even though the rest of the world did—or at least those who knew about what happened. Wendy Madigan had done a good job of covering it up to most of the world.

The six people he'd saved that day—what must they think of him? Surely he was a hero to them. If I had time, I'd look them up next week. Maybe they could shed some light on what had happened to Talon over there.

I finished my sandwich and wine and took my dishes to the kitchen—or rather across the room. My little studio apartment was cozy but comfortable. I was making a decent income now, and I'd be able to save up for a down payment on a car pretty quickly. Once I did that, I'd be able to move to a better place.

I grabbed my cell phone when it rang. My father. We hadn't talked in a while. He wasn't one for phone calls, just the occasional text checking in. My nerves jumped. If he was calling, it was probably not for a good reason.

"Hey, Dad," I said. "What's going on?"

"Hi, sweetie."

"Are you okay?"

My father cleared his throat. "I'm fine, Jade."

"Then why are you calling?"

"It's your mother. She's been in an accident."

My heart raced. There was no love lost between my mother and me. I'd last seen her a couple of weeks before, when she and her current boyfriend had been in Grand Junction. She had treated me to an expensive dinner, let me swim in her swanky five-star hotel pool, and that was that. She'd said goodbye with an air kiss to my cheek.

"Oh my God, is she okay?"

"I don't know all the details yet. But it doesn't look good, sweetie."

"What... Where is she? Is she back in Iowa with her boyfriend?"

"No, she's in Grand Junction. I figured you'd want to go to her. I'm driving out first thing tomorrow."

"You don't have to, Dad. I can take care of this. She's my mother. She's not your wife anymore. She hasn't been for a long time. You really don't owe her anything."

"I know. And you don't owe her anything either, Jade. But I loved her once, and she gave me the greatest gift in the world. You. And I want to be there for you, sweetie."

I breathed a sigh of relief. Having my strong father here would make this a lot easier. "Okay, Daddy," I said. "What hospital is she at? I'll leave now."

"Valleycrest," he said. "All I know is that she's been badly injured, and she was in surgery when I got the call a few minutes ago. I wish I could be with you tonight."

"Don't worry about that, Dad. I'll be fine. I love you." I

ended the call.

My first instinct should've been to call Marj. She was my best friend in the whole world, and she was the one I always went to when I needed someone. But I didn't want Marj right now. I wanted her brother.

Talon.

Not the optimal way for him to meet my mother, but I needed him with me. Would he come if I asked? Only one way to find out. I punched in his number.

"Hi, blue eyes."

"Hi," I replied.

"What's up?"

"I need to see you. Please. Can you go to Grand Junction with me tonight?"

"I've had a rough day, blue eyes. Why do you need to go to the city tonight?"

"I'm so sorry you had a bad day. I truly am. But I need you. My mother... She's been in an accident. She's at Valleycrest Hospital in Grand Junction. In surgery. I've been told it's not looking good. That's all I know."

"Oh, baby, I'm so sorry. Of course I'll come with you."

My heart leaped. "I can drive to the ranch and pick you up."

"No, I'll come and get you. I don't want you driving when you're upset. I'll be there in about a half hour."

"What about Roger?" I asked, referring to Talon's cute little mutt. "Marj is in the city tonight too."

"I'll text Ry to let him out in the morning. Don't worry. He'll be fine."

"Talon, thank you so much. Thank you," I whispered into the phone, my body numb.

I sniffed, my eyes moistening, but couldn't yet bring myself to cry for a mother I didn't even love but who still meant something to me.

"You okay, blue eyes?"

I sniffed again. "Yeah."

"Everything will be all right. Now you stay put. I'll be there before you know it." Silence. Then, "And I love you."

My heart doubled in size. "I love you too, Talon."

★ ★ ★ ★

We hadn't said a lot during our drive to the city. As we pulled into the hospital parking lot, Talon dropped me off at the entrance. "Go and see what's going on. I'll find a space and be right in."

I shot from the car, walking briskly in. I stopped at the registration desk. "I need to find my mother. Brooke Bailey."

The woman typed into her computer. "I'm not seeing anything."

"She was in an accident."

"Then you have to check with the ER."

"But she's in surgery! Surely you must—"

"I'm sorry, ma'am. You need to check with the ER. Down the hall to your right."

Could she have been any ruder? I turned quickly and nearly ran down the hallway.

The ER was full, of course. I had to wait in a fucking line of people. If my mother had been admitted, why didn't the hospital have a record of it?

Talon arrived about ten minutes later, when I was finally the next in line to talk to the receptionist.

"Anything yet?" he asked.

I shook my head. "I'm still waiting to find out what's going on."

The person ahead of me took a seat, and the receptionist nodded to me. "Yes, may I help you?"

"I'm looking for my mother. Brooke Bailey. She was in an accident." God, I didn't even know what type of accident it had been. I had assumed a car wreck.

The receptionist typed on her computer. "Yes, she's in surgery."

"What happened? Is she okay?"

"I'm afraid I can't tell you any more than that. You'll have to talk to her doctor."

Talon stepped up. "This is ridiculous. This is her daughter, for God's sake. Can't you give her any peace of mind at all?"

The receptionist's hard eyes softened as she raked her gaze over Talon. "I wish I could, sir. I understand how she must be feeling."

"Surely you can type into your computer and tell us what Ms. Bailey is having surgery for, can't you?"

She smiled, and for a moment I thought—

"I'm sorry, sir. I'm not allowed to give out medical information. You'll have to talk to the doctor or nurse. I'll let the charge nurse know you're here, and she'll be out to talk to you as soon as she can." She looked to me. "What's your name, young lady?"

"Jade. Jade Roberts. I'm her daughter."

She typed something on her keyboard. "Just find a seat. The nurse will be with you shortly."

Talon heaved a sigh. "Fine. We appreciate your help."

He took my arm and led me to two empty seats. We were

surrounded by sniffling kids and moaning adults, but I couldn't bring myself to care.

My heart beat a rapid staccato. Did I actually care about my mother? This was news to me. Tears choked me, and I fought a war inside my head and heart. I wanted to cry for her. Why?

Talon squeezed my hand. "Okay?"

And the dam burst. The tears I had been holding back flooded my eyes. I hiccupped softly, willing myself not to break down. Talon pulled a red bandana out of his pocket and handed it to me.

I wiped my eyes and blew my nose.

What was wrong with me?

The answer was clear. She was my mother. She had given me life, and I had to be grateful for that. But for her, I wouldn't be here sitting next to the man I loved.

Talon held my hand, and we sat silently until a woman wearing green scrubs walked toward us.

"Ms. Roberts?"

"Yes. I'm Jade Roberts."

"You're here about Brooke Bailey?"

"Yes. I'm her daughter. What can you tell me?"

"She was in a head-on collision. She was in the passenger seat of the vehicle, and her airbag didn't deploy."

I gasped. "Who was driving?"

"A friend of hers. He wasn't injured badly. Just got the wind knocked out of him by the airbag and some minor bruises, possibly a broken rib. He's been discharged."

"And my mother?"

"Severe lacerations, contusions, and abrasions. Broken knee, ribs, bruised pelvis. Possible internal and brain injuries.

Right now the doctors are trying to get her stabilized."

Brain injury? "Oh my God."

Talon squeezed my hand.

"Luckily she was wearing her seat belt. Otherwise she'd be dead."

"Why didn't the airbag..." I couldn't wrap my mind around this.

"We don't know, ma'am. Airbags aren't foolproof."

"Who was she with?"

"A man. Nico Kostas. He's up in the surgery waiting area, I think."

"That's her boyfriend." I breathed. "They had no record of her at admissions."

"They should. Though sometimes it takes a little while for our databases to update. She was admitted about two hours ago. We called the person in her wallet identified as an emergency contact. A Brian Roberts."

"That's my father. He's driving up tomorrow. He lives in Denver."

"You two can wait with her friend up in surgery. Come on. I'll have someone take you up there."

Talon rose and helped me up. We followed the nurse to an orderly. The young man took us up the elevator and across a hall to a waiting area.

Nico sat, his head in his hands. He wore a navy-blue tailored suit and a black-and-red tie, which was still tied at his neck. Shiny black leather shoes. I approached him.

"Nico, hello."

He looked up. "Brooke's daughter?"

"Yes, Jade."

"Of course. Jade. My mind isn't working very well at the

moment."

"I understand." I looked to Talon. "This is my—" My what? My friend? That would be insulting. My boyfriend? We weren't in high school. My lover? "Talon Steel."

Nico turned and regarded Talon for a moment before holding out his hand.

"Nico Kostas." He shook Talon's hand and then raked his fingers through his coal-black hair.

"What happened?" I asked.

Nico shook his head. "It's all a blur. We were driving down Stetler Road after dinner. It was quiet, and all of a sudden out of nowhere, a truck plowed into our lane and hit us head on. The other driver wasn't injured at all, like me. I don't understand what could have happened with the airbag. I..." He squeezed his eyes shut, and a tear emerged.

"It's not your fault," I said, hoping I was speaking the truth.

He opened his eyes. "I'm glad you're here. I can't stay any longer. I have to catch a flight back to Des Moines, and I'm already running late."

"You mean you aren't staying?" Did he care so little about my mother?

"I wish I could. But I can't get out of this. Brooke will understand."

Maybe Brooke would, but I sure as hell didn't. "Fine. Have a good flight." I took a seat.

Talon sat down beside me as Nico left the waiting area.

"Nice guy, huh?" I said to Talon.

"Maybe he does have somewhere to be," Talon said, "although..."

"Although what?"

Talon pursed his lips. "He seemed beside himself with

worry and concern when we got here, and now all of a sudden he takes off?"

"That's what I was thinking," I said. "But I don't have time to worry about her boyfriend being an ass. I need to find out about my mother."

"She's been in surgery for a while. Someone is bound to know something soon." Talon smiled.

God, his smile. He smiled more now. When I first met him several months ago, getting a smile out of him had been like pulling teeth out one by one.

Talon stood. "I'm going to find something to drink around here. Do you want anything?"

I wasn't thirsty, but I did need to go to the bathroom. "No, but could you stay here a minute in case someone comes out with any news? I need to use the restroom."

He sat back down. "Sure."

I kissed the top of his head and headed out to find the bathroom. As I turned the corner into a different hallway, I stopped.

At the end of the hallway stood Nico, talking to— Was it Larry? I squinted. It was a long hallway, but damned if it didn't look like my boss, Larry Wade. What the hell was he doing here?

The man who looked like Larry turned, met my gaze, and then pulled Nico around the corner. I walked swiftly and then began running, but by the time I reached the end of the hallway, the two men had vanished.

Had it been Larry? Had it even been Nico? My senses weren't functioning all that well. My knees buckled. What was going on?

I leaned against the wall and breathed deeply. When I

finally made sense of my environment, I turned and found a ladies' room.

A few minutes later, I walked back to the waiting area. Talon still sat, leafing through a sports magazine.

"Any news?"

He shook his head.

I sat down next to him and fidgeted.

"What's wrong?" he asked.

"Nothing. I just thought I saw..." What? My mom's boyfriend talking to my sleazy boss? So what?

"Saw what?"

"Nothing. I'm fine." I couldn't deal with what I'd seen and what the implications might be. Right now, I had to deal with my mother.

"Will you be okay for a few minutes? I'm going to go and find that drink. You want anything?"

I shook my head.

He returned a few minutes later with a bottle of Coke and sat down. He put his arm around me, and I snuggled into his shoulder.

And waited.

About an hour later, a woman in scrubs approached us. "Ms. Roberts?"

"Yes?"

"I'm Dr. Rosenblum, your mother's orthopedic surgeon. Her trauma surgeon, Dr. Melvin, is still in surgery with her."

"Is she all right?"

"She's holding her own. She's a strong lady."

"What's going on, then?"

"She has a shattered knee and a severely bruised pelvis. She's lucky she didn't break her pelvis. That's a six month recovery. She also has several fractured ribs. I've repaired the knee as best I can, but she may require a knee replacement if my repairs don't take. But right now, her bones are the least of our concerns. She had some internal bleeding. Dr. Melvin is finishing those repairs now. He'll be out to see you when he's done."

"Was he able to stop the bleeding?"

"Yes, we think so. He'll be able to tell you more when he comes out."

"Then that's good, right?"

She pursed her lips. Her head didn't move. No nod. No shake. "Yes, for the internal bleeding, but Ms. Roberts, your mother is in a coma. She may have a brain injury."

"What?"

"We'll have a neurologist do a thorough evaluation once she's stable."

"Once she's stable? Do it now, for God's sake."

Talon tugged at my hand. "Jade—"

I pulled my hand away. "No, Talon." I regarded the doctor. "Do it now. Do everything you have to do."

"Ms. Roberts, please believe me. We're doing everything we can right now." Her eyes spoke the truth.

"Does my mother have a chance?" I asked.

She smiled. "From what I've seen, I think she has a good chance. But Dr. Melvin— Oh, here he is now."

A large man in scrubs walked up to us. He held out his hand to me. "Ms. Roberts?"

I nodded.

"Jim Melvin. Your mother is stable for now. She's being transferred to the ICU for the rest of the night. We'll reevaluate in the morning."

I gulped. I should be asking questions, but none came to the surface.

"She'll get the best care here," Dr. Rosenblum said soothingly. "I can't tell you not to worry, but at least get some sleep."

"I want to see her."

Dr. Melvin nodded. "All right. But only for a minute. And I have to warn you, she has a lot of contusions and lacerations. She won't look normal to you."

The doctors led me to the ICU and into my mother's cubicle.

I gasped. She was hooked up to myriad machines, and her skin was gray and pasty. Her lips were cut, both eyes were blackened, and one was so swollen that the eyelid had turned inside out.

"She may require some facial reconstruction eventually," Dr. Rosenblum said. "But obviously we're more focused on keeping her alive right now."

Her heart monitor blipped slowly. "Why is her pulse so slow?" I asked.

"It's the anesthesia," the doctor said. "It's fine. As the drugs wear off, it will go back up to normal. She's on a lot of pain meds right now—"

A buzzing soared into my brain.

"Shit," Dr. Rosenblum said. "Crash cart!"

The buzzing turned to beeping—from my mother's machines. My heart beat in tandem with the equipment. My skin turned to ice.

"You're going to have to leave," the doctor said, ushering me out.

"But my mother!"

"We'll do all we can for her." She pushed me out the door.

CHAPTER FOUR

Talon

In a daze, Jade stumbled back into the waiting room. I stood and rushed to her.

"What's wrong?"

"My mom is crashing. Or something. They wouldn't tell me. Her monitors started blaring. I don't know."

I crushed her to me. I wanted to hold her and protect her from all that was wrong in this cruel world. I hadn't been able to protect myself, but goddamnit, I would protect her from the evil and cruelty that surrounded all of us.

But I couldn't. I had no control over what happened to her mother. I hadn't been able to save my own mother, and I couldn't save hers either.

She wilted against me, and I helped her sit down. All we could do now was wait.

A half hour later, the female doctor came out.

Jade stood. "My mother?"

"She's stable," the doctor said. "For now."

"Thank God." Jade wilted back into her chair.

"You need to get some sleep, Ms. Roberts. You're no good to your mother like this. Go home. I promise we'll call you if there are any changes."

"She's right," I said.

"No." Jade shook her head. "I don't want to go."

"Then let's at least get a room nearby for the night."

She sniffed. "All right. But I don't want to be more than a couple blocks away."

"We can handle that, blue eyes." I turned to the doctor. "Thank you for your help. Do you have our contact information?"

"Just leave it at the front desk when you go."

I nodded and walked Jade to the elevator.

It was going to be a long night.

★ ★ ★ ★

"Two rooms," I said to the guy at the front desk of the Carlton.

Jade held on to my arm, her eyes glazed over. I handed the guy my credit card, signed, and took the key cards.

Both on the fifth floor. Good. "Okay, come on, blue eyes." I led her to the elevator and pushed five. When we stepped out, I turned right to the first room. I slid the key in the slot and opened the door.

"Here you go. This is your room," I said.

She turned. "What do you mean, *my* room?"

I knew what was coming. "Your room. Mine is down the hall."

"Oh, no. You're staying with me. I need you tonight, Talon."

"Baby, you know I can't do that. Remember what happened the last time I slept with you?" I'd never forget, waking up and finding my hands around Jade's neck. I couldn't risk that happening again. Even though I'd worked through it with my therapist, I still wasn't ready to sleep with her.

I couldn't take the chance of hurting her.

She shook her head vehemently. "No. Please. No."

"I'll be right down the hall. I promise. If you need me, just call me."

"Talon, please. This is my mom. I didn't think she meant as much to me as she does. This is surprising me how much I'm freaking out. But all of a sudden, I want my mother so much. My dad is on his way. He'll be in sometime tomorrow." She looked down at her watch. "Okay, sometime today, but it won't be until later. He's driving in from Denver. Please."

"I can't, blue eyes. I can't take the chance."

She yanked on my arm, pulling me inside. The hotel door closed, and she grabbed my cheeks and pulled me down into a kiss.

The kiss was violent. We'd had kisses like this before, yes, but this one was different. Jade was so...*needy*.

Usually, I was the needy one.

I wasn't used to anyone needing me. Sure, my brothers and Marj said they needed me, but they didn't. Not really. No one had ever needed me the way Jade did now.

She clung to me as though her life depended on it, and then she broke the kiss with a gasp. "Please, Talon, don't leave me. I'll never ask you for another thing. I promise."

Something in her eyes made me stay. She was scared, genuinely afraid of losing her mother, whom I'd never heard her say a kind word about. But sometimes emotion ran so deep a person didn't even know it was there. I, of all people, understood that.

I nodded slightly. I'd stay, at least until she fell asleep. The room had two beds. I could sleep in the other, or I could go to my own room. Yes, I'd have to go to my own room. But later.

"Please"—she started sobbing—"I can't be alone tonight. I just can't."

"Shh," I said against her hair. "I won't leave you, baby. I'm here for you. Whatever you need."

Truer words had never crossed my lips. I was here for her, and I would do whatever she needed me to do. All she had to do was ask, and I would be there. I knew this in the depths of my soul.

She pulled back a bit, her steely blue gaze meeting mine. "I need you to make love to me, Talon. Love me. Show me what's really important in life."

We hadn't been together since I'd taken her anal virginity and freaked myself out in the process. But now was not the time to think of myself. I needed to think of Jade, put her needs above mine.

I *wanted* to put her needs above mine.

This was a new feeling for me. I'd spent so much of my life balled up in a spiral of self-pity that I never considered what others around me might need. Sure, I put in my work at the ranch, I did my duty overseas. I'd always done what was expected of me, but I never worried about benefiting anyone other than myself.

Jade had pierced my veil of self-pity, had crawled right under my wall.

But had she really crawled under? Had she cracked it open?

Or had I let her in?

No one had been able to tackle the wall until Jade—not my brothers, not my sister, not anyone. But Jade had gotten in.

I wanted her in. Would she still love me when she knew everything? She'd said as much. And she'd shown me, the last time we were together, just how much she trusted me. No one had ever offered me that level of trust before, not even my men overseas. They'd had to trust me. Their lives had depended on it. But they didn't know me from Adam. They were forced to trust me because I had been their commanding officer.

But Jade... No one was forcing her to trust me. She had given me her trust of her own free will.

What a gift that was.

I would not let her regret it.

I tightened my arms around her, squeezing her to me, cocooning her in a hug that I hoped was powerful and comforting. Just having her this close made my dick hard, as it always was when I was around Jade.

I loosened my hold on her and tipped her chin up so her blue gaze met mine. "Are you sure, baby? It's okay if you just want to go to bed and cry. I'll hold you. You can cry all night if you want to."

She shook her head. "I imagine I'll do my share of crying. But right now I want to make love. Please, Talon, show me what's beautiful in the world."

Pure love filled my heart. "*You* are what's beautiful in the world, Jade."

A tear streamed down her cheek. "I wish I could believe that. So much is going on."

"What do you mean? What's going on besides this?"

She shook her head again. "I don't want to talk about any of it now, Talon. Please, just take me to bed."

I wanted to know what was bothering her other than her mother, but my dick twitched in my jeans, and I also wanted to thrust inside her wet heat.

I led her to the bed, where I undressed her slowly. She was

wearing jeans and a T-shirt. She must've changed after work. I unclasped her bra and let it fall to the floor. Her beautiful full breasts fell gently against her chest. Her nipples were already pert and hard for me. I had to resist the urge to reach forward and pinch them the way that she loved.

I whisked her lacy underwear over her narrow hips and down her long and shapely legs. She stepped out of them and stood before me naked. Vulnerable. She reached forward and began to unbutton my shirt. When she got to my waistline, she pulled the shirt out of my jeans and then brushed it over my shoulders to the floor. She unbuckled my jeans and then unzipped them, pushing them down over my ass and hips. My cock sprang out, as hard as I'd ever been for her. She knelt and licked the tip, sucking off a drop of pre-cum. I had to stop myself from exploding right there. Then she stood and pushed me down on the bed, where she removed my boots, socks, jeans, and underwear. Then she sat down on my lap.

"Kiss my nipples, Talon." She held out her breasts.

Her nipples were brownish-pink, already tightened into hard knobs. I flicked my tongue over one. She sighed—that breathy whisper that drove me mad. I was hard beneath her, and I longed to thrust my cock up into her. Instead, I rained tiny kisses over one areola and lightly trailed my fingers over her other nipple. She sighed again, moving her hips, sliding her wet pussy over my cock.

"You tell me what you want, baby," I said against her soft flesh. "Anything, blue eyes. Just tell me what you need."

She moved her hips upward and then sank down on my hard cock. "I need *you*, Talon. Just you."

I let out a groan, my mouth still against the softness of her breast.

"That's it, baby," I said. "Just take what you need."

I resisted the urge to thrust upward. I let her go at her own pace, her own rhythm. She closed her eyes, sighing again. I looked up. My God, she was so beautiful. Her dark lashes lay like a soft curtain against her opulent skin. Her cheeks were a beautiful raspberry color all her own. Her golden-brown hair was in disarray, falling in tousled strands around her creamy shoulders. Her breasts were swollen and flushed, the nipples still taut, still begging for my touch. I leaned forward and caught one in my mouth, sucking as she continued to undulate.

"Talon, show me. Show me what's beautiful."

I repeated what I'd said earlier. "You're what's beautiful, baby. Only you."

One of her hands drifted down, and she began fingering her clit. I clenched my teeth, willing myself not to come prematurely. Watching her touch herself drove me crazy. She was so beautiful, so sensual.

She began moving faster. As much as I wanted to plunge up into her and explode, releasing, I held off. I wanted to give her what she needed, and I wanted her to take what she needed from me.

She had said those words to me the very first time we made love. And looking back, though I didn't know it at the time, it *had been* making love. She had offered herself to me without condition, telling me to take what I needed from her.

Now I was offering the same to her. I wanted her to take what she needed from me.

She increased her tempo a bit, riding me, losing herself within me. Her pussy was so sweet over my cock, gloving me as perfectly as it always had. I slid my hands over her thighs, up her sides, and then back down and grabbed the cheeks of her ass. I couldn't help myself. I began moving her up and down faster, faster, faster...

"Oh, yes," she said. "Just like that. Just like that."

I tensed, determined not to come until she'd had her release. She rubbed her clit furiously, moaning, writhing, until—

"Yes! Yes, Talon, I'm coming!"

I thrust upward into her. "Yeah, baby, come for me. Come all over me."

She continued riding me, pushing her pussy down upon me, and I felt every convulsion on my ultra-sensitive cock.

Her climax went on and on, until I could no longer hold out. I thrust up into her, aching to touch the most secret part of her, to possess her, and I released into the woman I loved.

She fell against my chest, her skin warm and covered with a sheen of perspiration. We clung together, both still releasing, warming within each other, joined, as we should be.

We both breathed rapidly, the scent of sex thick in the air. She made no move to get off me, so after a few minutes I leaned down, pulling her onto the bed so we were both lying down, still joined.

"I love you," I whispered against her forehead.

I didn't know if she'd heard me. Her eyes were closed, and she didn't say anything. She needed sleep. I held her, basking in her, for about a half an hour more before I moved myself away from her. Gently, I lifted her and covered her with the sheet and blanket. I brushed my lips softly over hers. "Good night, my love," I said. Then I went to the other side of the room.

I got into bed. I missed Jade's warm body next to mine, but I was not going to sleep with her until I knew there was no chance I would have a dream and try to hurt her again. I was a little apprehensive about even sleeping in the same room with her, but I couldn't allow her to wake up and find me gone. Not tonight.

Today—or rather yesterday—had been a major breakthrough for me. I'd told Dr. Carmichael something—admitted something to her in the actual words—that I'd never told anyone before, not even my brothers.

The time had come to open up to my brothers. And to my sister. Jonah was right. Marjorie had the right to know why she never got to know her mother. I texted all three of them, asking them to come to the ranch house on Sunday, where we could all have a talk. Then I texted just Jonah and Ryan.

It's time to tell Marj.

CHAPTER FIVE

Jade

I bolted upright in bed. Something had woken me. Where was Talon?

I sat, my mind jumbled and confused. Then a pounding on the door. Was that what had woken me?

I stumbled out of bed, naked as a jaybird. Luckily this was the Carlton, and lush white robes hung in the bathroom. I threw one on and then went to the door and looked out the peephole.

Talon.

I opened the door. "Where have you been?"

"I'm sorry. I went down the hall to make a few phone calls. I didn't want to disturb you. Forgot to take a key."

My heart raced. "How could you leave me? You knew I needed you."

"Baby, I was in the next bed. I was on alert all night. I just left for a little while."

"What time is it?"

Talon smiled and walked into the room. He went to the curtains and opened them. The bright sunlight nearly blinded me. Was it morning?

"It's one o'clock in the afternoon, Jade. You slept for twelve hours."

My heart popped out of my chest. "What? No."

"Yes. I had to call the front desk and get a late checkout. We don't have to be out of here until three."

I ran around the room, picking up my clothes. "But my mother. I have to go see my mother!"

"Blue eyes, your mother's fine. I called the hospital this morning and got an update. She's still unconscious, but she's stable."

I felt a little more relieved. "Still, I need to go to her."

"Do you want me to book you a room for tonight?"

"My father's coming today. I don't know what his plans are." Hurriedly, I grabbed my phone. Yep, sure enough, there was a text from my dad.

Should be at the hospital by three p.m., sweetie.

I turned to Talon. "He'll be here in a couple hours. He'll meet us at the hospital."

He shook his head. "I have to get back to the ranch, blue eyes. I wish I could stay."

My stomach dropped. "Please. I can't be alone."

"You won't be alone, Jade. Your father's coming. I'll stay until he gets here."

Tears clogged my throat. "No. I need *you*, Talon. You."

He sighed and pulled me to him, stroking my hair. "All right, blue eyes. If you need me to stay, I'll stay for a little while."

"Thank you."

"I want you to take a shower. I'm going to get us some food, okay?"

I shook my head. "No, we have to get to the hospital."

"I told you, there's been no change. She won't even know you're there, baby. Please, you have to take care of yourself too."

He was right. I nodded against his shirt. "All right. But it will be a quick shower. I want you back here in fifteen minutes."

He mock saluted me. "Yes, ma'am."

After Talon left, I started shaking, my nerves overcoming me. *No, Jade, keep it together.* I shed my lush robe and took a quick shower, letting the tears fall. I probably looked like shit anyway from crying yesterday, so what did it matter? Talon would see me at my worst. I'd obviously seen him at his worst, and I still loved him more than anything.

I hadn't brought a change of clothes, so I had to wear the ones I'd worn yesterday. Icky, but I had no other option. Once I got dressed, I went back to the bathroom and combed through my wet hair, deciding against the blow-dryer. I'd let it air dry. Then I grabbed my purse and put on a little bit of lipstick. That was it. I didn't have the energy for anything else.

Talon returned on schedule with burgers and fries. They tasted like sawdust, but my stomach appreciated it.

As much as I wanted to grab him and take him back to bed, lose myself and escape reality, I held myself in check. I had to get to my mother.

Once we got there, though, I found that Talon was right. She was stable, and there'd been no change. The most I could do was sit with her for a few minutes. They wouldn't let Talon in with me, so I sat alone, holding her hand that had a pulse oximeter clipped to it.

I wanted to say something to her, even though I knew she couldn't hear me, but I didn't know what to say. We'd never been close. She'd never cared enough to be close to me. The one time she'd come back, when I was fifteen, her second husband had cheated her out of her entire fortune from her modeling days. She came back to my father and me stone broke, and neither of us wanted anything to do with her.

I'd never regretted that choice. She hadn't been there for me during my formative years when I needed her. She had chosen her career over me, and that still burned. But she was my mother, and I did not want her to die.

So that's what I would say. I took a deep breath and squeezed her hand. "I'm sorry this happened to you, Mom. I really am. But I'm here. Dad is on his way. Nico had to fly to Des Moines. I'm sure he'll be back soon." Somehow, I knew that wasn't true. Nico wasn't coming back. But I couldn't say that to my mother, even if she was unconscious. "I know we were never close, but you are my mother. And in my way, I do love you."

A nurse came in to check her vitals.

"How is she doing?" I asked.

"She's doing as well as can be expected. I heard you talking to her. I think that's good."

I bit my lower lip. "She can't possibly hear me or even know I'm here."

The nurse smiled at me. "I've been working ICU for fifteen years, and I've seen a lot of patients like your mother. The ones who do the best are the ones whose family members sit with them, hold their hands, and talk to them, just as you're doing now. She knows you're here. You can bank on it."

Did she? Did she care? A couple of weeks ago, she had invited me to have dinner with her and Nico. I'd figured she was making an obligatory gesture. Had it been more than that? Now that I was an adult, did she want to try to repair our relationship? Better question—was I open to that?

My once-beautiful mother, now bruised and battered and fighting for her life, lay in silence. And the answer emerged in my mind. Yes. I did want to mend the relationship if possible.

The nurse finished checking my mother's vitals and went on to the next patient. I closed my eyes and sat quietly, still holding my mother's hand.

"Hey, sweetie."

I opened my eyes. My father stood in the doorway. I dropped my mother's hand, rose, and ran into his arms.

"Daddy, I'm so glad you're here."

"Me too. How's she doing?"

"They say she's stable, but she's unconscious, and she has a shattered knee, fractured ribs, and a bruised pelvis. And of course she looks like shit."

My father chuckled against my hair. "Poor Brooke. If only she knew what she looked like right now."

I couldn't help but return my father's chuckle. It was the God's honest truth. My mother hated not looking her best.

"You know, I don't think Brooke ever really knew just how beautiful she was," my father said. "We did have some good times."

I pulled back a little from my father and regarded him. His blue eyes, so much darker than mine, were sunken and sad. My dad had dated over the years, but he had never remarried. Was it possible he still held a torch for my mother? He had rushed out to be here by her side, but I'd thought that was because of me. My father adored me, so it was probably true. But had he also come out because of Brooke?

"You never talked much about her," I said.

He shook his head. "No. I couldn't. The emotion was too raw for a while, and then I didn't want to talk about it because of you, sweetie. I didn't want you missing your mother any more than you already did."

"But *you* missed her. I never knew."

"I had to be strong for you. One day, when you have your own child, you'll understand."

I gulped. "Obviously my mother didn't feel the same way."

My dad gripped my shoulders. "Listen, Jade, you are everything to me. And I know that's the way you'll feel about your own kids. Your mother did the best she could in her own way. She was just never satisfied with who she was."

"She ran out on me to be a supermodel. She could have done both. Didn't she know that?"

"I'm not sure she did. I said just a minute ago that Brooke never realized how beautiful she was. I meant that in more ways than one. She was never satisfied with anything. She thought she wanted to be Brooke Bailey, supermodel, instead of Brooke Bailey, wife and mother. It never occurred to her that she could be both, that she was good enough to be both. She was never satisfied in her career either, and as gorgeous as she was, she never thought she looked her best."

Thinking of that famous blue swimsuit poster my mother had made when I was a teen, I shook my head. "That's unbelievable. She's freaking beautiful."

My father sighed. "Even strapped down in the hospital bed hooked to all those machines, her face a mangled mess, she is still Brooke Bailey. And she is beautiful."

I looked into my father's eyes, and I saw more than just sadness there. I saw the way I looked at Talon and the way he looked at me. I saw love. My God. How could I have been so blind to it?

My father was still in love with my mother.

I sniffed. "I'm surprised they let you come back here. They told me only one person could be back here at a time."

"They told me the same thing, but I begged and pleaded, said I was her husband and that she needed both me and her daughter. Little white lie never hurt anybody."

Yes. He still loved her.

"Why don't you stay here for a little while, Dad? I have someone waiting for me."

"Do you? No one was there when I came through the waiting area."

"He probably went to get a soda or something. He loves Coke."

"Jade, are you...seeing someone?"

What a loaded question. I hadn't even realized I never told my father about Talon. But heck, I hadn't told Marj—my best friend and his sister—for the first couple months. I'm not sure why, but I just didn't feel like I could go spreading the news about it.

"Yes, actually. I'm seeing one of Marj's brothers."

My father widened his eyes. "They're so much older than you are."

Wow. I hadn't seen that coming. There was a lot about Talon that he could object to, but I hadn't even considered the age difference. If that bothered him, everything else about Talon was sure to give him nightmares.

"Actually, I had only met two of her brothers, Jonah and Ryan. I'm dating the middle brother, Talon. Remember? He was overseas while Marj and I were in college."

"And how old is he, Jade?"

I fidgeted, looking away from my father's gaze. "He's thirty-five."

"You're twenty-five."

"Yes, I know, Dad. I've done the math."

"That's a big difference."

"You were six years older than Mom."

He sighed, sitting down next to her. "True. And you see how that worked out."

"Mom was eighteen when she had me. She was just too young. She wanted a career. There's a big difference between an eighteen-year-old girl and a twenty-five-year-old woman."

My dad smiled. He was still so handsome. His eyes were dark midnight blue, so different from the light blue that I got from my mother. But his hair? It was the same as mine, only with a few streaks of gray at the temples. Golden brown and thick. He was about six feet tall, only slightly taller than my mother.

"Yes, and you've got a better head on your shoulders than she ever did. That's for sure. But don't you think this is a little soon after the whole Colin thing?"

The whole Colin thing. What a mess that had turned into. "You know what, Dad? I'm so sorry you lost all that money on the wedding, and if it's the last thing I do, I'll make sure you're paid back every single penny."

"Don't worry about that. It wasn't your fault."

"I know that. But I don't think I was ever really in love with Colin. It was more of a habit with us after a while. I think things happened the way they needed to happen. I just wish I had been the one to realize it first."

"Well, if you're sure it was the right thing."

"I am. And that's because I've met someone amazing."

He sighed. "All right."

"Look, if you're worried about Talon, why don't you come out to the waiting area and meet him? He's probably back by now."

"I'll meet him later, sweetie. I want to sit with Brooke for a while. You take a break. Get yourself something to eat or drink."

The look on my father's face was one I'd never seen before—sadness, worry...love. He needed to be here right now, holding my mother's hand.

"Okay. If you need me, just text. I'm not leaving the hospital, at least not until tomorrow night. I'll have to go back to Snow Creek to go to work on Monday."

"I'm making this an open-ended stay," my father said. "We have some projects in the works, but I trust my men to take care of them. They know the situation."

I smiled. "It will be nice to have you here for a while." Then I clamped my hand over my mouth. "Not that I think it'll take a while for her to recover. I didn't mean—"

"Jade, it's okay. I know what we're dealing with here. I want to be here with you and Brooke."

I nodded. "Text me if you need me." I left the ICU and headed back to the waiting area. Snuggling up to Talon, feeling his warmth—that was what the doctor had ordered for me, what I needed. My father might need to hold my mother's hand. I needed Talon.

But he wasn't in the waiting area.

CHAPTER SIX

Talon

My phone beeped. I knew before I looked that it was Jade responding to my text.

What do you mean you're leaving? You said you'd stay.

I let out a breath. I was a coward, truth be told. And I told her as much.

I'm sorry, blue eyes. I'm just not ready to meet your father yet. I'm...scared.

A few moments passed before my phone beeped with her response.

Fine. Do what you need to do.

Was that said with understanding or resentment? Damned texting. I decided not to ask.

I'll be back tomorrow evening if you need a ride back to Snow Creek.

Again, nothing for a few minutes. Then, *Don't bother. My father can drive me back.*

All right.

I stopped typing for a moment. The three words that had been so difficult for me to say now hovered on my fingertips. Why was it easier to say them than to type them into a text? I forced them from my fingers.

I love you.

I waited a few minutes, but she didn't respond. No "I love you" back. Not that I blamed her. I was running out on her when she needed me. I had to get back to the ranch. I had told the guys and Marj to meet me tomorrow, and this was something I had to do. And there was truth in what I'd told her. I wasn't quite ready to meet her father. Yes, I loved Jade, and yes, I wanted her for life, but I had so much more to get through myself before I could meet the man who'd raised her, who'd helped shape her into the amazing person she was. Right now, I still wasn't good enough for his little girl. He would see right through me.

An hour later I arrived back at the ranch. I had a text from Marj.

Got your text. I'm staying in Grand Junction tonight. I want to go to the hospital and see Jade and her mom. What time do you want to meet with the guys and me tomorrow? I'll make sure I get back.

I texted her back. *How about lunchtime?*

Cool. I'll be home by noon. But don't expect me to cook.

No worries. I'll have Felicia make us up something and leave it.

Then I texted the guys.

Marj will be home at noon tomorrow. Can you guys come over at eleven?

It was time.

★ ★ ★ ★

I slept fitfully, though that was nothing new. I'd texted Jade a few times to check in. She sent me back robotic texts with no "I love you."

I didn't blame her. Once I got through everything, she would understand. I just hoped she'd stick around long enough.

Jonah and Ryan arrived right at eleven. I had already poured myself a Peach Street.

"A little early, huh, Tal?" Ryan said, joking.

I heaved a sigh. "There's a reason I wanted you guys to come early. Before we tell Marj, I need to tell you guys exactly what happened."

Ryan smiled. "We're here for you."

Jonah gripped my shoulder. "Yes, we are," he said.

I took a big sip of my whiskey and let it singe my throat. "I am. It won't be easy for me to say, and I'm going to tell you right now, it won't be easy for you guys to hear. But I made a breakthrough in my therapy on Friday. And it's time."

"If you're sure," Ryan said.

My little brother. Always having my back. Never wanting to push me. I was his hero. For the first time, as I thought about that, I felt that maybe his faith in me was not misplaced.

"I'm ready. I owe this to you guys. And to myself. Pour yourself a drink if you need one and then meet me on the deck."

I walked out the French doors in the kitchen to the gorgeous redwood deck. Instead of sitting down at the table, I took one of the chaise longues beside the hot tub. I at least wanted to be comfortable if I was going to do this. For a moment, I was sitting in the hunter-green recliner in Dr. Carmichael's office. Gripping the wooden arms of the chaise longue wouldn't feel as good against my hands as that supple leather.

Jonah and Ryan came out—Joe with what looked like a gin and tonic, Ryan with a can of soda.

"Sorry," he said, when I eyed the can. "I'm just not ready

for alcohol at eleven."

I nodded. After all, he wasn't the one about to divulge his guts.

"I asked you guys to come before Marj gets here because I can't tell her everything. Not the worst of it. But I need you guys to know a few things. I may not tell you everything, but you deserve to know what happened. And you deserve to know what happened to Luke."

Jonah widened his eyes. "You know what happened to Luke?"

"Yeah."

Luke Walker had gone missing a couple of weeks before I had. He was my age, skinny little kid with buckteeth, a basic nerd. He wasn't a close friend of mine, but for some reason I had decided to save him from the bullies who were always after him. And then one day Luke disappeared. My first thought was that the bullies had taken him, but they hadn't. Jonah's best friend was Bryce Simpson, Luke's cousin, and the three of us and Ryan decided to try to figure out what had happened to Luke.

I cleared my throat. "The day I was taken, I saw Luke."

"Was he alive?" Ryan asked.

I let out a breath. "No, he was already dead." I paused a moment, getting my bearings. "That old shack where two of the guys were, they had Luke in there. I don't know what they had been planning to do with him so close to his home or whether my presence changed their plans. He was already dead but..."

"But what?" Jonah asked.

I closed my eyes, but the image swirled like a kaleidoscope inside my head. "They hacked him up with an ax. They... They made me watch, threatened to kill me if I screamed or threw up."

I opened my eyes. Both my brothers' faces had turned pale as ghosts. Neither said a word. What was there to say?

"They put what was left of his body into a giant trash bag. I don't know what they ultimately did with it. They shoved it in the back of a pickup, tied my hands and legs, and shoved me in the backseat. I think I was in and out of consciousness as we drove. I don't know how long we were driving."

My brothers still stayed silent.

"It's hard to remember the details. I think it was dark outside by the time we got to wherever we were going. Seemed like we had been driving for hours."

"Tal," Jonah said, his voice cracking, "if you'd been driving for hours, how did you make it back home when you escaped?"

I shook my head. "I have no idea. So much of it is a blur. We'll get to my escape in a while. But for now, I need to tell you what I told Dr. Carmichael."

My brothers nodded.

"They pulled me out from the back of the truck and unbound my feet. They pushed me into an old house and down the stairs into a basement. I had wet my pants, but it didn't matter because they took my pants and underwear away from me anyway. All I had was my shirt and a ratty old gray blanket they gave me." I stopped, squeezing my eyes shut again.

"It's okay, Tal," Ryan said, his voice lower than usual. He was trying so hard to be strong for me. My little brother.

But it wasn't okay. Nothing about my life since then had been okay. If it was ever to be okay again, I had to get through this.

"There was another one at the house, also wearing a black ski mask. Remember, Ry, there were only two guys at the old shack off the Walker place."

Ryan nodded.

"Anyway, once I got out of the basement, I found out why I was there. They each..." I gulped. "They each...*raped* me."

My brothers' faces were unreadable. They didn't look surprised at my admission. But why would they be? Why else would three psychopathic degenerates keep a young boy prisoner for months? Surely they'd known, or at least guessed. I'd been taken to a pediatrician and poked and prodded after my return, so my parents must have known, even though I never spoke of it.

"Once they were done, I threw up. I couldn't help it. They left me, and I lay down on my blanket. What might've been a couple of hours later, one of them brought me a glass of water and a sandwich, along with an old paint bucket I was told to piss and shit in. I ate the sandwich and drank the water. Sometimes they tormented me with water, holding a really nice clean glass of crisp ice water just out of my reach. I still have nightmares about that sometimes. I still have nightmares about all of it."

Jonah cleared his throat. "That's perfectly understandable."

Of course it was. I looked to my older brother. "Now that you know the gory details, do you still wish it had been you instead of me?"

The question was unfair, I knew. But Joe had always wished he had been there to protect me. I wanted my brothers to be happy that this hadn't happened to them. I wouldn't wish that horror on either of them. I wouldn't wish it on anyone, except the three psychos who'd done it to me. On them, I wished all that and everything else hell had to offer.

And I was well acquainted with what hell had to offer.

"I don't really know how to answer that," Joe said.

"Just say you're glad that didn't happen to you."

He shook his head. "I can't."

I heaved a sigh. My older brother wrestled with his own demons. I knew that. I wished I could help him, but I couldn't do a damn thing for anyone until I helped myself.

"How did you escape?" Ryan asked.

"I don't really remember. Every once in a while they would leave the door open and dare me to run away. Every time I tried, of course, they caught me and punished me for it, so I stopped trying. One day, the door was open, and they hadn't come. I don't know if they had just forgotten to lock me back in or what. But I ran up the stairs wearing only my tattered T-shirt. I had no pants."

"But when you were found," Ryan said, "you were wearing your clothes."

"That's one of the things I can't figure out," I said. "I remember walking up the stairs, opening the door that had been left open a crack, running outside, and then scampering across the vast wilderness. And the next thing I remember I had clothes on and I was walking around the outskirts of Snow Creek."

"Maybe you blacked out," Jonah said.

"Maybe," I said, "but I was ten years old. Where would I have found clothes?"

Jonah rubbed his jawline. "Maybe you found a house and went to it and asked for clothes."

I shook my head. "No, that doesn't make any sense. Anyone who found me and gave me clothes would have alerted Dad. Or at least the police."

"True," Ryan said.

"Is there anything else you want to tell us about this?" Jonah asked.

"No. You can certainly infer the rest. It happened many times. I stopped counting. Why would I want to remember that number? Some things are a blur, but what isn't a blur is what they did to me. I remember every horrific detail of the pain and of the humiliation. And unfortunately, it has made me who I am today."

"You're wrong, Tal," Ryan said. "Those couple of months don't define you. You're a good person. You were a hero overseas, and you're a hero to me."

"Only because I saved you that day. And let me tell you, I'm fucking glad you got away."

Of course, my younger brother didn't respond. Neither of my brothers could ever admit that they were glad that this hadn't happened to them. I didn't understand, but maybe I wasn't meant to. They had their own issues that they needed to work through. Jonah especially. He shouldered a lot of guilt because of what happened to me that day. I'd tried to relieve him of it, but I had not been successful.

"How much of this are we telling Marj?" Joe asked.

I sighed. "Only the bare minimum. And definitely not the part about them butchering Luke. I don't want our baby sister burdened with any more than necessary. I'm sorry I had to burden you guys."

Joe shook his head. "No, Tal, we needed to know."

True. They did. In their own ways, they had gone through it with me. "Do you guys want to come to therapy sometime? Or go by yourself? I'm sure Dr. Carmichael would be happy to see you."

"Whatever you want us to do," Ryan said.

"Ryan," I said, "you have to quit leaving this all to me. I have finally decided it's time to work through this, and I'm going to do it—not just for you guys and not just for Jade but for myself. And you have to do the same. Maybe you didn't go through what I went through, but you're dealing with it in your own way. Whether you seek help has to be your decision, not mine."

Jonah cracked a bit of a smile. "You're a wise man, Tal."

Wise? Was he kidding? I was about as far from a wise man as any man on the planet. I shook my head.

"No, hear me out. It may have taken you a while, but you finally came to the conclusion that you need help. There's no shame in that, and now you know that. There's no shame in what happened to you. The shame belongs to the people who did it to you."

As I listened to Joe's words, I thought about Dr. Carmichael's words a few days before. She'd said that I understood objectively that none of this was my fault, and she was right. I did. The problem was not my conscious mind but my subconscious, and I would work through it.

"Hey, guys!" Marj called. She stepped onto the patio.

"Hey." I stood. "How's Jade's mom doing?"

Marj blew out a breath. "She's the same. Jade's going to be coming back later tonight because she has to go to work in the morning. She's a little miffed at you, though."

"I know. But she's with her dad, and there were a few things I needed to take care of here. She'll understand one day."

"Yeah? When?" My sister whipped her hands to her hips. She was a spitfire, that one.

I sighed. "Well, sit down, and I'll tell you."

Marj eyed the empty glass of whiskey sitting in front of

me. "Drinking at noon?"

"Yeah. But I'm done. I'm only having one."

She pulled up a chaise and sat. "What did you guys want to talk to me about?"

None of us spoke for a moment, but when Joe opened his mouth, I held up a hand.

"No, Joe. I need to say it." I turned to Marj. "You were right to be suspicious. We *have* been keeping something from you. And it's been my decision. Because what we've been keeping from you is something that happened to me."

"Oh my God. Are you okay?"

I cleared my throat. "I'm fine. Or at least, I'm getting there."

She went pale. "What do you mean? Talon, you're scaring me."

"You know those news articles you found in Joe's house? About the child abductions around the area twenty-five years ago?"

Her eyes got as big as dinner plates.

"One other child was taken, one that never made the news." I closed my eyes, willing myself to calm. "That child was me."

CHAPTER SEVEN

Jade

I had left my dad for a bit to go down to the cafeteria and get us some food. As I was walking back with some sandwiches, my cell phone buzzed with a number I didn't recognize. I was so tired and worn out, I considered not answering it, but my curiosity eventually got the best of me.

"Hello?"

"Jade?"

"Yes. Who is this, please?"

"It's Ted Morse again."

"How did you get this number?"

"I found it among my son's things."

My body went cold. "Has Colin shown up yet?"

"No," Ted said, his tone accusatory, "and it seems that you are the last to have seen him."

"I assure you I have no idea where he is, Ted." Worry tugged at me. I no longer loved Colin. Hell, I no longer liked him very much. But I didn't want anything to happen to him.

"I've contacted the police. They'll be in touch to question you since you were the last person to see him alive."

Alive? Did he think Colin was dead? My heart thrummed wildly. "That's not true. There were three other people with me the last time we saw him." I thanked God for the alibi of

Talon and his brothers. The way Ted was talking, I thought he might be trying to pin this on me.

"And who would that be?"

"Talon Steel and his brothers, Jonah and Ryan Steel. Colin and I had just come out of a restaurant, and the Steel brothers were coming out of a bar across the street."

Ted huffed into the phone. "Drunk, no doubt."

"No, they were *not* drunk. Also, it was Friday night and it was warm. There were other people walking around."

"And that's the last time you saw my son?"

I didn't like his tone. Ted Morse was a powerful man, and as an attorney, I knew better than to spill my guts like I had. "Ted, if you want to talk to me any more about this, you'll need to call back some other time. I'm in the hospital right now. My mother's been in an accident, and she's currently in ICU."

Silence for a moment. Then, "I'm sorry to hear that."

His tone didn't indicate sorrow at all.

"So I'm sure you understand why I can't talk anymore. Goodbye, Ted." I ended the call.

Marj had left a couple hours ago, promising to read Talon the riot act for leaving me here. I desperately wanted to call him just to hear his voice. Instead, I went back to the waiting room where my father sat. "There wasn't much down there. Here are a couple of ham-and-cheese sandwiches."

"Thanks, sweetie."

"No problem." I unwrapped one and took a bite. I didn't want to talk about Ted and Colin, so I said something else that had been on my mind. "I can't get over Mom's boyfriend leaving her here."

"That *is* weird," Dad agreed. "How much do you know about him?"

"Not much. She said he was a senator from Iowa. I've never heard of him. But it's not like I keep up with who the senators are in Iowa. Honestly, I'm not sure what Mom saw in him. He was good-looking enough, olive skin and a great head of hair, nice build. But he had a slimy look about him, you know? I can't really put my finger on it, but something about him seemed off."

"You didn't like him?"

"I can't really say that. All I did was have dinner and go swimming with the guy. He was perfectly polite to me, and he had a gorgeous tattoo—a phoenix on his forearm. You know I've wanted a tattoo for the longest time, and that image was just so apt for my life right now."

My dad shook his head. "I'll never talk you out of that tattoo, will I?"

I smiled. "Sorry, Dad. I'm going to be inked at some point. I don't know when, though. I had originally planned to come to the city this weekend and scout out some shops, but Mom's accident obviously superseded that intention."

"I'm sorry your mom is in here suffering, but if there's any good in it, it's that it kept you from getting a tattoo." He smiled at me.

"Only postponed it, Dad."

Talon had reacted horribly to the idea of me getting a tattoo. It was the image—the phoenix—that had upset him. What did he have against the phoenix?

I couldn't be concerned with that now. I was about to take another bite of my sandwich and then get back to the subject of Nico Kostas, when one of the new duty nurses came out.

"Mr. Roberts, Ms. Roberts, Ms. Bailey has regained consciousness."

I stood up quickly, knocking over my coffee. "God, I'm so sorry."

The nurse smiled. "Happens all the time up here. I can only let one of you in right now."

I looked to my father.

"You go, Jade. She's your mother."

I nodded and followed the nurse. My mother was still hooked up to all the machines, and her eyes were still slits, though the swelling had gone down quite a bit. Amazing what a difference a day made.

"She looks the same."

"She's conscious. Just say hello to her. Tell her you're here."

I took my mother's hand. "Mom?"

Her eyes fluttered just a touch.

"Mom, it's Jade. I'm here. You've been in an accident, but you're going to be okay."

Her eyelids fluttered again, and her lips started to move. I couldn't make out anything she was saying.

"It's okay. You don't have to try to speak. Just know that I'm here. Dad is here too. Everything's going to be fine."

She moved her lips again, and one word croaked out. "Nico."

I resisted the urge to roll my eyes in front of the nurse. Her daughter was here, her ex-husband was here, but the only person she wanted was the guy we hadn't seen head nor tail of since the first night.

"Nico will be here soon, Mom." It was most likely a damned lie, but I didn't want to upset her.

Her eyes flickered closed. I squeezed her hand, but there was no more response.

"It looks like she's drifted out of consciousness again," the nurse said, "but this was an excellent sign. The doctors are very happy with her progress."

I let out a sigh of relief. "Can I let my dad come in?"

"He's welcome to come in for a few minutes, but she's no longer conscious."

I went back to my dad and told him what happened.

"I'd like to meet this Nico," he said.

"I'm sure he'll turn up sooner or later," I said. "A bad penny always does."

★ ★ ★ ★

I was exhausted when I got to work the next morning. My dad had driven me back to Snow Creek at nine o'clock last night, and then he drove back to Grand Junction, where he was staying at a motel. I said a quick hello to Michelle and David and then sat down at my desk and checked my calendar for the day's events. I had a city council executive session this afternoon, but for now I was free. I took care of some administrative crap and then continued my investigation. I had fired up the Internet when Michelle poked her head into my office.

"Jade?"

"Yeah?"

"Have you heard from Larry today?"

I shook my head. "No. I haven't seen him since Friday." The ghost of him standing in the hallway talking to Nico drifted into my head. I was sure it had been Larry, though he hadn't been wearing shorts and flip-flops as he had been when I'd last seen him at the office. Of course, it had been near midnight when I saw him at the hospital.

"He hasn't called in, and I can't reach him on his cell or home phone. He's due in court in ten minutes, Jade. Can you cover?"

"What?" My stomach dropped.

"It's just the Monday-morning docket. You can probably find all the folders on Larry's desk."

"Are you kidding me? I'm not prepared—"

"It doesn't matter, Jade. You have to go. You're all we have right now."

I stood, flustered. "Fine, fine. Find everything in Larry's office to get me up to speed. I'll run over to the courthouse right now, and you bring the information as soon as you can. I'll tell the judge what's going on so I don't look like a complete imbecile."

The judge would probably not care that Larry had left me high and dry. She'd expect me there. The Monday docket was the Monday docket, and if the city attorney wasn't available to handle it, the assistant city attorney would have to. And that, unfortunately, was me.

I looked down at my casual khaki pants and silk camisole. Hardly courtroom attire. Had I known I'd be going to court, I'd have worn a suit. Fortunately, a black cardigan was wrapped around the back of my chair. It would have to do.

"Bring the information as soon as you can," I told Michelle again. "I'll head on over."

Damn Larry anyway.

★ ★ ★ ★

A few hours later, it was over. I'd received a good talking to from Judge Gonzalez about adequate preparation. She wasn't even slightly interested in the fact that her city attorney had flown the coop.

Judges were judges. I pledged to be better prepared from now on.

"Michelle," I said, when I returned to the office, "from now on I want to be advised of all cases. All court dates. Whether Larry is in town or not, I want them all on my calendar, and I want to be fully apprised of each one. Make sure I get that information, please."

I walked into my office and slammed the door shut. I hadn't meant to be rude to Michelle. This was no more her fault than it was mine. But getting a dressing down from a judge was never on any lawyer's "to do" list. Judge Gonzalez had been fair with me on Talon's case, and she was perfectly within her right to expect me to be prepared to take over the city attorney's duties. This would *not* happen again.

I sat down and picked up the receiver of my landline, ready to call my father, when my cell phone rang. Another number I didn't recognize. "Hello?"

"I'm looking for Jade Roberts."

"You found her. May I ask who this is?"

"Yes, this is Detective George Santos with the Denver PD. I'm investigating the disappearance of Colin Morse."

Oh, shit. Just what I didn't need right now. "I'm afraid I don't know anything about that."

"It's our understanding that you were the last person to see Mr. Morse."

"I was one of four to see him that evening. I was accompanied by three other people, and there were many others milling around the city on Friday night."

"We've been in touch with the Snow Creek police. All

three of them." He scoffed. "One of their fine officers of the blue will be coming to see you, Ms. Roberts."

"I will look forward to it with bated breath," I said sarcastically. I knew better than to get mouthy with a cop, but this was so not a priority for me right now. I wanted Colin to be okay, but I had too much else going on to be overly concerned. All I wanted to do was check on my mother and then go and see Talon once work was over.

Would it be too forward to call Marj and request one of her homemade meals tonight? I could sure use it. And I could sure use a heavy dose of Talon.

I was still pretty mad at him for leaving me there Saturday. But maybe he really wasn't ready to meet my father.

Maybe he didn't love me as much as I loved him.

The thought hurt, kind of sliced my heart in two, but Talon was Talon. Something was eating him up inside, and as desperately as I wanted to help him, he had to let me first.

I went to pick up the landline again to call my father when a knock sounded on my door. God, would this workday never end?

"Come on in," I said.

Michelle entered with an officer I recognized. "Jade, Officer Dugan needs to speak to you."

"Sure. Come on in, Officer Dugan." I gestured to one of my chairs. "Sit down."

"I'm here to—"

I held up a hand. "I know why you're here. I just got off the phone with the Denver PD. Go ahead and ask your questions. But I don't know much."

"I understand. When was the last time you saw Mr. Morse?"

"He took me to dinner Friday night a couple weeks ago. When we were coming out of Enzio's, the Steel brothers were coming out of Murphy's. We all chatted for a while, and then Colin went on his way."

"Chatted" wasn't really the right word for what had gone on, but I had basically told the truth. No punches had been thrown, thank God, though all four of them had threatened each other.

"Did he say where he was going?"

"No, he didn't. I assumed he was going back to wherever he was staying in Grand Junction. He told me he was going to show up for court Monday morning, but then he didn't."

"Were any words exchanged between him and Talon Steel?"

I was an officer of the court. I could not lie to an officer of the law. And there was no need to. We had lots of witnesses.

"Yes, words were exchanged."

"What kinds of words?"

"Talon wasn't happy to see Colin, obviously. And neither were his brothers. I don't really remember everything that was said."

"Did any of the brothers touch him in any way?"

I closed my eyes, trying to remember. Had Talon grabbed Colin? No. He and Jonah had both raised their hands to him, but they hadn't touched him.

Thank God.

"No, they didn't."

"Good." Steve looked visibly relieved. "What was the last thing Colin said before he left?"

"I don't recall his exact words, of course, but he said he would see me in court on Monday."

"And he didn't show up for court."

"That's right."

"Is there anything else you can tell me about this?"

I shook my head. "That's all I know, Officer."

"You can call me Steve." He smiled.

I smiled back. "All right, Steve. I'm Jade."

"Okay, Jade." His lip twitched.

Was he nervous?

"Uh...would you like to join me for a drink after work?"

CHAPTER EIGHT

Talon

"Yesterday we told my sister about what happened to me." I gripped the now familiar green leather arms of the recliner in Dr. Carmichael's office.

"And how did that go?" she asked.

"About as well as I expected. She was angry and hurt that we hadn't trusted her with the information before now. She asked a lot of questions, wanted to know a lot of details—details I wasn't comfortable sharing."

"And how did you handle that?"

"I didn't want to lie to her. I had only just shared some of the details with my brothers earlier. I didn't want to saddle Marjorie with the horror of it all. So I just said I didn't remember a lot of the details. She seemed to buy that."

"Why did you feel she couldn't handle the details?"

"I guess it's not that I thought she couldn't handle them. She's my baby sister. I didn't want her to *have* to handle them, you know?"

Dr. Carmichael nodded. "I understand. How else did she react?"

"She cried. She said it helped her understand so much now. And of course she wanted to tell..."

"Tell whom?"

"She wanted to tell Jade. Jade's her best friend."

Dr. Carmichael cleared her throat. "What did you say to that?"

"I made her promise not to tell Jade."

"And did she?"

"Yes, she promised, but on one condition."

"And that was?"

"That *I* tell Jade. When I'm ready."

"I think that's a good idea. I think you do need to tell Jade. But you don't have to be in any hurry."

"How can you say that? I'm in love with this woman. And she said she loves me too. I'm amazed every day at the fact that someone so wonderful could love me."

"That's exactly why I *can* say that, Talon. You have a long way to go to work through all of this. You need to understand that you're worthy of her love, and you're just not there yet."

Dr. Carmichael was right. I sure wasn't there yet. "You're right. I'm not."

"So is there anything you want to talk about today?"

Where to start? "I have no idea where to begin, Doc. So much happened, and so much of it affected me."

"The last time, you said that the one with the phoenix tattoo seemed to be the leader."

"Maybe that's a good place to start," I said. "The phoenix."

"What about the phoenix?"

"I came across a similar image recently."

"Oh? Where?"

I breathed in and let it out slowly. "Jade. She was going to have an almost identical image tattooed on her lower back."

Dr. Carmichael widened her eyes. "Really? How did that come about?"

I rubbed my temple, my head beginning to ache. "Hell if I know. She said she found the image in one of the books at our local tattoo shop in Snow Creek. I went over, and damned if the image wasn't nearly identical to the one I remember."

"Odd that Jade would pick the same image."

I nodded. "More than odd. She said the phoenix was a symbol to her. She got left at the altar and was humiliated, and the phoenix rising from the ashes pointed the way to a new and better life for herself."

"That does make sense," Dr. Carmichael said.

"It didn't make sense to me."

"It didn't make sense to you? Or were you just so upset by the image that you didn't even think about it making sense?"

God, I hated it when she was right. "That image...it's hard for me to..." I closed my eyes, gripping the arms of the leather chair.

★ ★ ★ ★

Again I focused on the colorful bird on his forearm—the only thing I could focus on to keep myself from screaming or emptying my stomach. It was a menace, but it was also my safe place.

"Yeah, boy, that's it, take it all," Tattoo said, pumping into me.

Low Voice and the other laughed, jeered. "That's it. Give it to him good. You know he likes to be fucked."

Again, I stared at the bird. I'd learned not to argue with what they said. Did they really think I liked this? How could anyone like any of this? I hated it. I hated it to the depths of my soul. But I did what I had to do to survive. The first few times, when I screamed, "No, I hate this!" I'd been punished with a beating.

Why did I try to survive? Most of the time I wished I were dead. But still, every time they came, I did what I had to in order to survive.

Every damned time.

★ ★ ★ ★

I opened my eyes. "That phoenix has been part of my life since then."

"How so?"

I swallowed. "I always thought I remembered every single horrific detail of what I went through. But honestly, Doc, new memories surface all the time. Like, for example, I just remembered about the one guy missing a toe. How could I have forgotten that?"

"Talon, your mind does what it has to so that you can survive. You were ten. It's only natural for you to block out some things."

"But something as innocuous as how many toes one of my captors had? Why would I choose to block that out, when I remembered so many of the horrors?"

"I don't know, but we *will* figure it out. You did remember the phoenix."

True. "For a long time, the phoenix was the only thing I remembered about the whole experience. Other than the abuse, that is. I'm afraid that has always been etched into my psyche. I wish I could forget it."

"Forgetting things and blocking things out come with their own problems," the doctor said. "The fact that you do remember is actually in your favor, as far as healing goes."

"I'm sure you know what you're talking about, but let me tell you, remembering all of that is a curse."

"The curse is that it happened to you. Remembering it will help you get through it."

"I hope you're right."

"Let's get back to the phoenix. That was the only thing you remembered about your captors. Why do you think that is?"

I had only just begun to solve the riddle of the phoenix. All those years had passed. I had named my horse Phoenix, for fuck's sake. I'd had a poster of a phoenix on the wall of my room. Yet the phoenix represented hell to me. "The phoenix was the one constant in everything, Doc. The one thing I remembered about the guy. When they were...attacking me, I wasn't allowed to scream, or I got beaten. I wasn't allowed to throw up, or I got beaten. Basically all I was allowed to do was take it like a man, as they liked to say. So I had to find something to focus on, and I focused on that phoenix on his forearm."

"So in a way, the phoenix became a haven for you."

"I don't know if I'd say that exactly."

"Why wouldn't you say that?"

"Because the phoenix represented the one who was the hardest on me, the one who was the meanest, the leader of the three. It was on his body."

"Yet it provided an escape."

"Maybe. It did give me something to focus on. And then, here's the weird thing. Five years later, when I turned fifteen, my dad got me this awesome horse. Black as midnight and sleek as suede. I named him Phoenix."

Dr. Carmichael twisted a strand of blond hair. "Really? Why Phoenix?"

"Honestly? I never really thought about it until recently.

It just seemed like the name fit."

"It may well have fit. But there's another reason you named your horse after an image you detested. And it's because you didn't detest it. Not entirely."

"No, I *did*."

"I'm not denying that. Part of you did detest it. It represented hell to you. But it was also your escape. And what better name for a beautiful black horse that could run like the wind, on whose back you could ride and escape?"

Wow. Epiphany. She was right. Deep in the marrow of my bones, I knew she was right, even though... "I just don't understand it."

"In time, you will. Trust me. It makes perfect sense."

"But when I was alone, at night in the dark, the walls seemed to close in on me. Sometimes they talked. I know it was in my mind, but it seemed so real at the time. And sometimes it wasn't just the walls. It was the phoenix who would talk to me, taunt me."

"That was the phoenix that represented hell. But the name you gave your horse was the phoenix that represented your escape."

"I do understand what you're saying, Doc. It really does make sense. But I don't understand how it *can* make sense. How can one image have two opposite meanings for me?"

"Because it had two opposite meanings for you at the time. It's a fairly common thing."

I gripped my jaw. "If you say so."

"It makes perfect sense, Talon. It makes perfect sense that you would name your horse—upon whom you probably rode fast and long and did a lot of escaping—after the one thing that allowed you some escape during your time in captivity, even if that thing also meant the opposite to you."

"I'd prefer it to have no meaning at all for me."

"I'd prefer that no one had to go through any kind of sorrow or mental illness in life. Of course, that would mean I'm out of business." She smiled.

I gave her a half smile back. "Touché."

"So you said Jade was going to get a tattoo, and it happened to be the same image."

"Yeah. Luckily, she only got the regular ink transfer done, and I told her no way was she going to get a tattoo."

"How did she react to that?"

"Not good. But that was the least of my concerns at the time. I tracked down the tattoo artist who did the original tattoo. But it's been twenty-five years, so he couldn't remember who he had done it on. He did say it was his original design though."

"But it's possible that someone else had done the same design or something similar."

"Yes, it's possible. But this was done in Snow Creek. And I was abducted in Snow Creek."

"I see. So you talked to the guy who did the tattoo."

"Yeah. Like I said, he couldn't remember. Said he'd been stoned most of those years."

"Did he keep records?"

"I have no idea. I asked him to check. He's supposed to get back to me. I'll lean on him a little."

"Well, that's a lead. Have you changed your mind about catching these guys? You seem to go back and forth."

I let out a sigh. "I honestly don't know, Doc. I'd love to see them pay for what they did to me. And as I've told you, I've had more than one fantasy about doling out my own idea of justice." I held up my hand. "Yes, yes, I know. I won't do it. I spent enough of my life in captivity. I don't want to spend the rest of it in prison."

"Good idea."

"My brothers really want me to try to find them. They'd like to see them locked up too."

"I would too," Dr. Carmichael said.

"I suppose I could put a few high-paid PIs on the job. God knows I have the money."

"Why don't you?"

Good question. Why didn't I? Better question. Why hadn't I? "You need to understand. It's only recently that I actually decided I could dredge this up and deal with it."

"I do understand. But now that we're working through it, maybe it's time to hire those PIs."

She was right. "Maybe it is time."

"Our time's about up for today, Talon," Dr. Carmichael said.

I grabbed my cell phone out of my pocket and looked at it. I had turned off the ringer during my session. I had a text from Jade.

I need to see you. I'm coming over after work.

CHAPTER NINE

Jade

I hadn't gotten a text back from Talon, but I drove out to the ranch anyway. I had tried to let Steve Dugan down easily. I'd told him I had just had a major breakup a few months ago and I wasn't ready to go out yet. I had desperately wanted to tell him I was seeing someone else, but Talon and I hadn't made our relationship public, and I wasn't sure how he felt about doing so. I figured we'd better talk about it.

Marj opened the door when I knocked. Something was off with her. She didn't look right.

"Are you okay?" I asked.

"Come on in," she said.

No answer to the "are you okay?" thing. "Marj..."

She sighed. "Just a rough day around here."

"Yeah? Is everything okay at the ranch?"

She bit her lower lip. "Yeah, just"—she sighed again—"a hard day. We have them sometimes. What are you doing here?"

"I came to see Talon."

"He's not home yet. I expect him anytime. You want a drink? I could sure use one."

"Sure. Whatever you're having is fine."

"I'm having a stiff scotch."

That was so not like her. "Marj, what the hell is wrong?

Have you eaten yet?"

She shook her head. "Felicia just left. Dinner's on the stove. You're welcome to some."

"What about you?"

"Not hungry."

Something was definitely wrong. "Spill it, Marj."

"I told you. I'm fine."

I gripped her shoulders. "Remember, best friends don't have secrets."

She poured her scotch. "God, Jade, I wish I could tell you."

"You can."

The back door opened, and Talon walked in. Roger rushed from my feet over to him, panting.

His eyes widened when he saw me. "Jade."

"Did you get my text?"

"Yeah."

"Then why do you look so surprised to see me?"

Marj jiggled her glass of scotch. The ice clinked against the glass. "That's my cue to leave. Dinner is on the stove, guys."

"Marj? What in the hell?"

"She's okay," Talon said.

"No, she's not. She's not eating. She's drinking scotch. She looks like hell. That's not the Marj I know."

"Trust me, blue eyes. She'll be fine. It was a rough day."

"Yeah, that's what she said. Why didn't you answer my text?"

"I was at an appointment. And then I just wanted to get home." He smiled, sort of. "How's your mom doing?"

"Better. And thank you for asking. She's out of the coma. I wish I could spend more time with her, but I'm glad my dad is there."

"I'm sure that gives you peace of mind."

I nodded. "We need to talk, Talon."

"Did Marj say something to you?"

"No. But she's keeping something from me."

"I'm sure she's not keeping anything from you." He dropped his gaze to his feet, went to the refrigerator, and poured himself a glass of iced tea. "You want something?"

"A glass of that tea would be great."

He poured me a glass. "So what do you want to talk about?"

I cleared my throat. "Steve Dugan asked me out today."

Talon's eyebrows shot up. "He *what?*"

"Simmer down. I told him no. In fact, I told him I had just gotten out of a long relationship and I wasn't ready to date. But the fact of the matter is, I wanted to tell him about us. I just wasn't sure I could. Can we...make our relationship public?"

"That's what you want to talk about?"

"Yeah. What did you think I might want to talk about?"

He sighed. "Me leaving you in Grand Junction the other night. Not meeting your dad."

I cracked a smile. "Well, yeah, that's on my list as well. And it's another one of the reasons why I wasn't sure I could make our relationship public with Steve. I mean, if you say you're not ready to meet my dad, what does that mean exactly?"

Talon sat down at the table and gestured for me to do the same. "Blue eyes, you may not believe this, but I have never met a woman's dad in my life."

"I'm sure you've met a lot of dads, Talon, and some of them probably had daughters."

He shook his head. "You know what I mean."

"Okay. So you've never met a girlfriend's dad."

"I've never had a girlfriend."

I froze, silent. Beads of condensation emerged on my glass of iced tea. I didn't know why I was surprised. He'd told me at the beginning that he used women, took what they offered and then went on. It would make sense he'd never had a relationship before.

"Well, my dad is really easygoing. He'll be great as a first dad." And hopefully as a last dad too. I didn't want to think of Talon meeting any other girlfriends' dads ever. I wanted to be his one and only girlfriend for the rest of his life. But it was way too soon to voice those thoughts.

"I have so much to work out, blue eyes."

"Can't you let me help you? I want to help you. I love you."

He closed his eyes. "I don't want you going out with Steve Dugan."

"Talon, I don't *want* to go out with Steve Dugan. But I need to know that you and I are moving forward. That we're in a real relationship. That what we have means something to you."

He opened his dark eyes. "How could you think it doesn't mean something to me? I told you I loved you, for God's sake. I've never said that before."

"I understand. I really do. And I'm so glad you love me. It means everything to me. But what are we to each other? Up until now, I haven't felt I could tell anyone that I'm in a relationship with you. Are you okay with that? If Steve Dugan or anyone else asks me out again, can I say I'm in a relationship with you?"

He took a sip of iced tea, seemingly lost in thought. He closed his eyes again. "Jade, I want a relationship with you more than I've ever wanted anything. I've told you this before.

You're the only thing I've ever wanted."

"You *have* me, Talon. So why do I feel like I can't tell people about us?"

"This is difficult for me. I've never..."

"You've never what? Been in a relationship? You've made that clear. What's the big deal here?"

He sighed and took another sip of his drink. "I've got so many things to work out, Jade. I don't know if I'm ready to go public with a relationship yet."

"Then what am I supposed to tell Steve Dugan or the next guy who asks me out? And Talon, men *will* ask me out." I added that last part for Talon's benefit. Frankly, I'd never been nearly as popular with the guys as someone as gorgeous as Marj was, but it wouldn't hurt Talon to think I was.

"I don't want men asking you out."

"How exactly are you going to stop them? This is a small town, and I'm new blood. If you're not willing to admit that you're in a relationship with me and men don't know that I'm taken, how do you expect to keep them from asking me out?"

"You can just say no. Tell them what you told Dugan. That you just got out of a long relationship and are taking it easy. That's even partially true."

"Or"—I braced myself—"I could just go out with the guys who ask me out."

His face reddened. "*What?*"

"You heard me. Steve Dugan is a good-looking man. He seemed pretty nice and straightforward. What would be the harm in having a drink with him?"

He stood and grabbed my shoulders, yanking me out of my chair. "You will not have a drink with Steve Dugan or any other man, here or anywhere."

"Are you forbidding me? Just like you forbade me to get a tattoo?"

His eyes blazed with fire. "Goddamnit, Jade, why the fuck do you do this to me?"

"Do what—"

His lips came down on mine. His tongue was cold from the iced tea, but still he tasted of Talon—sweet minty cinnamon. This was one of his raw kisses, one of his kisses that said I was his and only his.

If only he were willing to say that with words.

I pulled away with a smack. "Talon, we—"

His lips crushed onto mine again. No use talking to him right now. Talon was showing me something he didn't have to, something I already knew very well. That I was his. And I was willing to be his, his lover, his life partner even, if he wanted it that way. But I wasn't about to be told what I could and couldn't do.

I tried pulling away again, but his grip was too hard. We were suctioned together. So I let the kiss happen. Kissing Talon was no hardship. I loved every minute of it. Our tongues twirled together as he kissed me hard with passion, with fervor. His kisses were like a drug, something that got into my system and that I couldn't live without.

When he finally ripped his lips from mine and inhaled a deep breath, I tried backing away, but he held me fast. He nipped at my neck and then came up to my ear. "You will not go out with anyone. Do you understand me?"

Before I could answer, he slammed his lips onto mine again. And though I wanted to argue with him and tell him that he didn't own me, my body took over and I melted into his kiss.

Our lips slid against each other's, our tongues tangled and

dueled, my skin tightened around me, and my body heated. Sizzling arrows shot straight to my pussy. My nipples hardened and pressed into my bra. He held me tightly against him as he continued to devour my mouth.

You're mine, that kiss said. *You're mine and no one else's. Only I will possess you.*

And the kiss was right.

I didn't want anyone else.

His hard cock pulsed against my belly. I unclenched one of my hands from his upper arm and grabbed it.

He groaned into my mouth.

He broke the kiss, and again, before I could say anything, he lifted me into his arms and walked out of the kitchen swiftly.

I didn't bother to ask where we were going.

I didn't bother to resist.

He was taking me to bed, and no matter how much I hated the fact that he'd "forbidden" me to do anything, and no matter how much I wanted to make our relationship public, I would always go to bed with him. He didn't have to ask. He could take me by force, and I would go. I would never deny him.

This was solid truth.

When we got to his room, he kicked the door shut, walked through the sitting area and into his bedroom, and threw me—not gently—onto the bed.

"Get undressed," he said, his eyes dark fire, his skin aglow with perspiration. He raked his fingers through his heavy mop of hair, tousling it sexily.

Refusing him never crossed my mind. Slowly I pulled my camisole over my head and tossed it to the floor. Then I unclasped my bra and got rid of it as well. I cupped my breasts, holding them out in offering, thumbing my nipples softly.

They were already hard as red currants, longing for his lips. I pinched the right one and then the left.

Talon sucked in a breath. "God, blue eyes."

I was already turned on. My panties were no doubt soaking, and just a few little pinches to my nipples by my own hand got my motor running big-time.

Talon raked his fingers through his beautiful hair again. "I said, undress, Jade."

I bit my lower lip, and he sucked in a breath again. I lay down on the bed, slid my khakis over my hips and down my legs, and kicked them off along with my black pumps. Only my lacy thong separated me from total nudity.

I turned my head and met Talon's dark gaze. With my left hand, I squeezed my nipple, while I trailed my right hand down my abdomen, over my mound, and underneath the lace of my thong. My pussy was slick with moisture.

"I'm wet, Talon," I said. "So wet."

"God..." He pulled my thighs to the edge of the bed, spread my legs, and ripped my thong off me, tearing it and throwing it to the floor. He inhaled between my legs. "God, blue eyes, you smell so ripe. So ripe for me."

I closed my eyes and sighed, waiting for his tongue to stroke my wet folds.

But his tongue didn't come. I opened my eyes and lifted my head a bit, meeting his fiery brown gaze.

"This pussy is mine, Jade. You hear me? Mine."

Well, it was one step closer to me being his. Maybe he wasn't claiming all of me, but he was at least claiming my pussy.

"Yours," I said. "This is your pussy."

"Damned right it is." He swiped his tongue from my asshole all the way to my clit.

I shuddered. Blood boiled in my veins. One touch from this man, and I was liquid, molten.

"You taste good. So fucking good. Apples, peaches..."

He ate my pussy, the succulent sounds drifting to my ears, turning me on even more. As he ate me, I brought my hands to my breasts and played with my nipples. God, so good.

He forced his tongue inside my channel and then moved to my clit, sucking it between his lips until I was sure I would implode, but then he turned back to my slit, and he pushed my thighs forward and tickled my tight little hole.

"Such a sweet little asshole, blue eyes."

This time he flicked his tongue against the sensitive flesh. I was on edge. So ready to come. I twisted my nipples further. If only he would go back to my clit just for a moment. But that would mean his tongue would leave my asshole, and that would be a problem indeed. Two tongues—if only he had two tongues...

When he breached my tight hole with a finger, I jerked, almost ready to come.

"You like that, baby? You like when I fuck your little ass? It's so sweet, baby, such a sweet little butt."

I pinched my nipples harder, twisting them almost off. What I would give for those nipple clamps...

And then two fingers entered my pussy. He thrust his hand in and out of me, filling both holes.

When his lips came down on my clit, I unraveled, soared to the stars and back, still twisting my nipples. God, so good. So fucking good.

When I finally came back to earth, he was still moving his fingers in and out of my pussy and my ass. I didn't want him to stop. It still felt so good.

I opened my eyes, and he was looking at me, his eyes black with smoke.

"That's right, baby. Twist those nipples. Make yourself feel good."

"Kiss my pussy some more, Talon. Please. Eat me. Suck me."

He lowered his head and swiped his tongue over me, his fingers still buried inside. I could come again so easily, but I wanted to kiss him, taste my juice on his lips.

I sighed, letting him do whatever he wanted. If he wanted to fuck my ass again, I would let him. He could do whatever he wanted to me. I was his.

"God, baby." He stood and removed his burgundy shirt. It landed in a wine-colored puddle on the floor. His chest was as beautiful as ever, dark hairs scattered over the copper coin nipples, ripped abs, and that lovely trail of black hair leading to paradise. He unbuckled his jeans and slid them and his boxers over his narrow hips. His gorgeous cock sprang out at attention.

"I'm going to fuck you, Jade. Spread your legs. Show me my pussy."

I was only too happy to comply.

Within a few seconds, that glorious cock was inside me, and Talon was thrusting, thrusting, thrusting...

"God, Jade."

One more thrust, and I was soaring again, reaching to the moon as I climaxed around him.

"That's right, baby. Come for me. You come for me. Only for me."

He pumped and he pumped and he pumped, and with one loud groan, he slammed home.

I was so in sync with him that I could feel every pulse as he shot his semen into me.

He collapsed on top of me and then rolled over onto his back. His jeans were still around his knees, and his boots were still on.

"God, Talon," I said, "that was amazing."

He turned to me, his eyes still blazing. "Blue eyes, we're not even close to done."

CHAPTER TEN

Talon

My cock was hard for Jade again almost instantly. Amazing how I could have her and then want her again so quickly. She was so beautiful, lying there, her legs still spread, her body glistening. Her nipples were red and ruddy from her own hands. How I longed to suck them between my lips, to make her scream. Her hair was fanned out in a golden-brown curtain on the bed, her silver-blue eyes heavy-lidded. Her mouth was red and swollen from our kisses, and she licked her lower lip. So fucking sexy. And her pussy, engorged, the color of red wine...

I loved eating her, finger fucking her, playing with her ass. I longed to take her in that tight hole again, but I hadn't performed very well when I'd taken her ass for the first time. Maybe that hadn't been such a good idea, given my history. Still, everything had gone fine until—

I didn't want to go there right now. I wasn't done making love to her yet, and damn it, nothing would take that away from me.

She was mine. No one else could have her. No one else would take her out. Anyone who tried would answer to me.

Only I would possess her.

I propped up on my side and gazed at her body once more. I reached toward her and caressed her taut abdomen, her beautiful, mountainous breasts. As I fingered one nipple, it hardened under my touch.

She closed her eyes and sighed, that sweet sigh that could only come from Jade's lips.

"Mmm," she said. "That feels so good."

I wanted her to feel good. I wanted her to feel so good that she couldn't remember ever having been with anyone else, that she would never want to be with anyone else again.

I sure as hell didn't.

So why was I so afraid of making our relationship public? Declaring to the world that Jade Roberts was mine?

Maybe because that also meant that I was hers?

That wasn't a problem. I didn't want to be with anybody else. But could I saddle her with the mess that was my life?

Not yet.

I watched her slow inhalations, the slow rise and fall of her beautiful chest. She was my everything—everything I had ever wanted and the only thing I'd ever wanted.

And—as unreal as it seemed—she actually wanted me.

She wanted to make the relationship public. Wanted the world to know about us.

I hardened like a rock. I wanted her again.

I nudged her. "Come here, baby. Sit on my face and suck my cock."

She smiled, moving slowly to do as I bid. When she sat that sweet, succulent pussy down on my face, I almost exploded right then and there. She was so beautiful, so red and swollen, so juicy and tangy. I lapped her up like a cat lapping milk. So wonderful. She undulated her hips, smearing her pussy all over my face. God, it was hot. Then she leaned forward, taking my cock into her moist, warm mouth.

The more she sucked my cock, the more I wanted her pussy. I licked, her taste only getting better as she sucked my cock deeper into her throat.

She groaned against my cock, sexy little vibrations that drove me insane. All the while, I sucked at her, ate at her, shoved my tongue far into her. Then I moved to her asshole, flicked my tongue in and out of the hot little rosette.

I lifted her off me to inhale. "That's it, baby. Ride my face. Suck my hard cock." And then I shoved my tongue into her once more.

I reached forward and grabbed a handful of her sweet tits. I found her nipple and pinched hard.

"Ah," she groaned against my cock, her pussy exploding around my face.

I was drowning in her juices, and oh, sweet Jesus, what a way to go. I couldn't get enough of her. I sucked and I sucked and I sucked, aching to infuse my total body with her essence.

I pinched her nipple once again, and she climaxed around me again. God, how I loved it. I sucked at her clit, tongued her wet cunt, licked her little asshole. She squirmed over me, drenching me in her sweetness.

I wanted to make her come again, bathe in her succulence one more time, but I couldn't hold off much longer. I had to have her, and I wanted to come inside her again.

I lifted her hips from my face. "Baby, turn around and sit on my cock. I want you to ride me."

She complied. She always did. In the bedroom at least. She turned around, and oh, how beautiful she was as she sank onto my cock. She covered me so completely, gloved me so grandly.

"Ride me, baby. Ride me and touch yourself so you come

again."

I reached forward and grabbed both of her nipples, pinching, while she trailed her hand down to her vulva and started rubbing her clit.

She rode me slowly, so fucking slowly that I thought I was going to go insane, but I couldn't make her stop because it was so crazy good. Excruciatingly good.

"Talon, feels so good, baby."

"Yes," I groaned. "Ride me faster, baby. Faster."

She obeyed me, as she always did. Her pussy sank down on me and then up, down, up down, up, down in a whirlwind, so fast, so hard that I exploded, my whole body convulsing.

I closed my eyes, pinching both of her nipples. Words escaped my mouth, but I didn't know what they were.

All I saw was rapture, nirvana, Jade and me circling a kaleidoscope and spiral of wantonness and pleasure.

The climax went on and on, and as she kept rubbing her clit, she joined me in the rapture, coming again.

She kept pistoning, up down, up down, driving me insane. When she finally slowed down, we were both panting, sweat covering our bodies, our hairlines damp with perspiration.

She clambered off me and lay down next to me on her back. "My God, Talon. That was incredible."

"Yeah, sure was, baby."

"You make me feel so amazing," she said. "I do so love you."

I propped up on my arms and looked over at her. "I love you too. Now, tell me you're not going out with Steve Dugan or anyone else."

She shot up. "Are we really back to that again?"

"Why not? That's what started this."

She shook her head. "Talon, you will never learn, will you?"

"Learn what?"

"That you don't own me. I don't want to go out with anyone else. But if you're not willing to make a commitment to me, why shouldn't I? You're going crazy about this. Just like you did about that damned tattoo."

"Which you will not be getting," I said.

She shook her head again. "Do you hear yourself? You don't control me."

"Seems like I control you just fine in here."

"This is the bedroom, Talon. And I like submitting to you in the bedroom. It's a turn-on for both of us. But I will not be a submissive in any other facet of our lives. I'm my own person."

"What if that's the kind of relationship I want? A submissive not just in the bedroom but in every facet of our lives?"

She regarded me, her steely blue eyes both angry and sad. They misted over, glazing with tears. "If that's truly what you want, I'm afraid I'm not the woman for you."

She gathered her clothes, quickly dressed, and walked away.

Don't let her go, Talon. Don't let her go.

She was everything I wanted. The only thing I had ever wanted.

Was I ready? Was I ready to truly make her mine?

CHAPTER ELEVEN

Jade

This wasn't ending. I knew that. At least, I didn't think it was. But Talon had to understand that he didn't own me, that I had a right to my own life. If I wanted ink on my body, I would have it. And if he couldn't commit to me, I had every right to—

Oh, hell. Who was I kidding? I didn't want to date Steve Dugan or anyone else. I only wanted Talon. Feared I'd want no one but Talon for the rest of my life.

As I neared the kitchen, warm hands caressed my shoulders. Hot breath whispered into my ear.

"Don't go."

I turned into Talon's warm embrace. I didn't say anything at first, just let him hold me. He clung to me as if he were afraid I would disappear.

"Please don't go," he said again.

I pulled back from him a bit. "I don't *want* to go, Talon."

"Then don't."

"But you're asking me to be someone I'm not." I turned him around, and slowly we walked back to his bedroom, into the sitting area. I sat down on his couch and motioned for him to sit next to me.

"I love making love with you, Talon. I like submitting to your desires. It's what I want to do in the bedroom. I want you to take what you need from me. That's how I show you my love, how I show you my trust. But I also show you my love in other ways. I'm not asking you to be something you're not. Yes, I'd like to go public with our relationship, but if you're not ready, we won't."

"That's not exactly how you put it, Jade. You said if we don't go public, you'll just go out with whoever asks you."

I giggled. I couldn't fault him for that one. "Talon, I'm not going out with anybody else. I don't want to."

"Then why did you say that?"

I shook my head. "I don't know. I guess because I get tired of you forbidding me to do things. I'll be your submissive in the bedroom, but I won't be your slave."

"I never asked you to be my slave."

"Not in so many words, but when you forbade me to get a tattoo—"

He stood, pacing, clearly nervous. "That tattoo..."

"What about the damned tattoo, Talon? Why did you react so violently about it? So violently that you went down to the tattoo shop and paid them off not to tattoo me?"

"You don't know that."

"Oh, come on, give me a little bit of credit. Why else would they turn away good business?"

He sighed and sat back down. "Okay. You're right. I made sure they wouldn't tattoo you."

"You realize you can't pay off every tattoo shop in Colorado, don't you?"

"Jade"—he took my hand—"I'm asking you. Please, if you love me, don't get that tattoo."

His eyes showed his seriousness. I saw a sadness, a determination, a hardness.

"If it means so much to you, I won't get that particular tattoo. Maybe I could find another image of a phoenix that I like."

He squeezed my hand, hard. "Please, Jade, not a phoenix."

I gulped. "Why? Can you tell me why?"

He shook his head.

"Talon, I know that there's a lot bottled up inside of you, and I haven't even begun to explore all of it. I know all of that, yet I love you. This obviously means something to you, is important to you in a way that I don't understand. Please, if you love me, please tell me why you don't want me to get a phoenix tattoo."

"I can't."

"It doesn't make any sense. Your horse is named Phoenix, for God's sake."

"There are things. Things I just can't explain to you now."

"Will you be able to explain them to me at some point?"

He turned to me, took both my hands in his, his eyes serious. "I hope so, blue eyes. I sincerely hope so."

★ ★ ★ ★

Back to work the next day, and still Larry didn't show. I ended up in court again on a domestic violence case that I had no clue about. I felt bad that I had been short with Michelle again. It wasn't her fault he hadn't shown up.

Once I got back, I was able to call my dad and check in on Brooke. She'd had a few other bouts of regaining consciousness, but they hadn't lasted long. The way work was going, with Larry nowhere to be found, I wouldn't have time to go visit Brooke until the weekend.

Near the end of the day, Michelle came to my door and told me the mayor was here to see me.

"Sure, send him in." I had no idea what was going on, but the assistant city attorney certainly didn't turn down the mayor.

A tall man with silvery hair and blue eyes entered, dressed casually in jeans and a polo shirt. Even Larry hadn't dressed that casually, except on Fridays, when he came in wearing shorts and flip-flops sometimes.

"Jade"—he held out his hand—"I'm Tom Simpson."

I remembered his name from the article I had read about Talon's homecoming and heroism. I stood and shook his hand. "It's nice to meet you. What can I do for you?"

He gestured to my chair. "Please, have a seat." He took a seat opposite my desk. "Have you heard from Larry Wade at all?"

I shook my head. "Last time I saw him was Friday when he left the office." I chose not to tell him that I thought I might've seen him at the hospital in Grand Junction later that night. I couldn't be sure it was him, so why rock the boat?

"We've all been trying to get hold of him," Simpson said. "But since no one seems to know where he's gone—not his ex-wife, not his kids, not anyone—I need to make some changes in this office."

Shit, was I about to be fired? Not that I relished this job too much, working for such an unethical bastard, but it was putting money in my pocket for the time being. "Understood. What needs to be done?"

He smiled. "As of tomorrow morning at eight a.m., you are the acting city attorney, Ms. Roberts."

I widened my eyes. "I am?"

"I've talked to Judge Gonzalez over at the courthouse. She's informed me how well you've taken care of Larry's cases, having been thrown into them with virtually no preparation."

Really? After the dressing down she'd given me? "Thank you. I've already made arrangements to keep apprised of everything on the city's docket, just in case something like this happens again."

"I'm glad you've done that. It'll make your transition a little easier."

"I appreciate your confidence in me, Mayor Simpson."

He smiled. "Please, call me Tom. We don't stand on ceremony around a small town like Snow Creek." He stood. "Oh, and by the way, there's a $10,000 pay raise in it for you."

"Wow. Thank you. I do appreciate that, though it's not necessary."

"Well, we certainly wish it could be more, Jade, but as you know we're a small town. The city attorney is normally an elected position, although I appointed Larry when the previous city attorney retired in the middle of his term. If you choose to run when the current term is up, you may certainly do so. If you're elected by the people, you will get substantially more."

I did some rapid calculations in my head. That new car was coming closer and closer. I secretly hoped Larry would stay away for a long time.

"When is the term up?"

"Next year."

"Well, I'm sure he will be back soon."

"That won't affect your position, Jade. Unless he has a damned good reason for taking off, I intend to see his resignation when he returns."

"You do know, Mayor...er...Tom, that I'm a brand-new attorney."

"Yes, I'm aware of your credentials. But as I said, Judge Gonzalez has been highly complementary of your performance the last couple days. And we are a small town. It won't take you long to get up to speed on everything." He smiled and stood. "I'll let you get back to your work." He turned and left my office.

I leaned back in my chair. Was this a good thing or bad thing?

Common sense told me it was a good thing. I could take over as city attorney. I could whip this office into shape. There would be no more ethics-bending with me in charge. Plus, it was a pay raise, and I could certainly use the money. The sooner I got together a down payment for a new car, the sooner I could move into a better place. Plus my student loans were coming due anytime now. Yes, all in all, this was a good thing.

So why were the hairs on the back of my neck standing up?

CHAPTER TWELVE

Talon

I was going to have to give poor Axel a raise. He was a great foreman at the orchard, and I had not been pulling my weight lately, always driving into Grand Junction for therapy. Today was no different, although I had gone in early to meet with Robert Prendergast, also known as Biker Bob, who was the designer of the infamous phoenix tattoo that Jade wanted to have inked on her body for all time. Despite my throwing a few more Benjis his way, he hadn't been able to find the records of who he had done the tattoo on twenty-five or so years ago.

Now, here I sat in the dreaded hunter-green recliner, gripping its arms as usual. "It's strange," I said to Dr. Carmichael. "I've been coming here now for what...several weeks? I've had countless sessions. And still, I dread this each time." I looked up at her. "No offense."

She chuckled. "No offense taken. Therapy isn't easy, Talon. I'm sure you know by now it's no walk in the park. It's normal to dread your sessions. But tell me, how do you feel after you've had a good session?"

"I feel..." How did I feel? I had never really stopped to think about it. I'd been living in a haze for so long. My times with Jade were the only times I was even close to at peace. But when I considered it, thought about how I felt, especially after that session where I finally admitted that I had been raped, a weight had been lifted off my shoulders. "Honestly, I can't say I feel good exactly, but I feel that I'm carrying less of a burden. Does that make sense?"

She smiled. "It makes perfect sense. And as we move forward, you will feel good eventually when you leave here. I promise."

I hoped she was right. I could really go for feeling good. The only times I felt good were with Jade, and she wouldn't be around forever.

Or would she?

"Doc?"

"Yes?"

"Do you think I'm capable of having a real relationship?"

"You mean with Jade?"

I nodded. "It's what I want more than anything. She's the only thing I ever wanted. And she wants to make our relationship public."

"And you don't want to?"

I twisted my lips. "It's not that I don't want to. Sometimes I want to scream from the top of my roof that she's mine, all mine. But then I think about how unfair that would be to her. What do I have to offer her?"

"You have yourself. I have a feeling that's really all she wants."

"But you know what I've been through. I'm broken. I'm not sure I'll ever be whole."

"Are any of us ever whole?" the doctor said. "Everyone has his own burdens to bear, Talon. Granted, most people don't have the kind that you have. But there's an old saying that if everyone threw their problems in a pile, and you saw what they all were, you'd go racing back to take your own."

I couldn't help a small chuckle. "Seems unlikely that I would take my own problems back."

"Maybe," she said, "but remember, everything you've been through in your life has made you who you are today. And who you are today is the person that Jade fell in love with."

I sat for a moment, letting that sink in. I'd never looked at it that way before. "I always thought that if she knew who I truly was, her feelings for me would be different."

"Just because you haven't told her everything that happened to you doesn't mean she doesn't see you for who you really are. She knows there's something inside you, something you need to work through. That part is obvious to anyone close to you. And she hasn't run away from it, has she?"

I shook my head. "No, she hasn't. Even when I begged her to."

"It's never possible to know every single thing about the person you fall in love with. Everyone has a few things he keeps to himself. That's normal."

"But if you get into a relationship, one that's supposed to last forever, aren't the two supposed to become one?"

"One in that they're unified, as a partnership, but the two people are still individuals. That never changes. In fact, if that starts to change, those are the times marriages tend to fail, when one tries to bend for the other."

"I can't imagine Jade bending." I let out a laugh. "In fact, we just kind of had a discussion about that."

"You want to tell me about it?"

I hadn't really come here to talk about my relationship with Jade. There were other things more pressing. But what the hell? "She doesn't like it when I forbid her to do something."

Dr. Carmichael slid her lips into a grin. "That's pretty understandable from where I'm sitting."

"But you don't understand. In the bedroom..."

"What?"

"In the bedroom, she does whatever I ask her to. Whatever I command her to."

"Lots of women enjoy taking a submissive role in the bedroom. That doesn't necessarily translate to a submissive role in the rest of her life."

"That's exactly what she said."

"I've said it before. She sounds like a smart woman."

"Yes, she is that. Definitely. That's part of what I love so much about her. She's hot, don't get me wrong. Gorgeous, even. But her brain is just as sexy."

Dr. Carmichael smiled again. "Most women would love to meet a man who feels that way."

"I need to ask you something, something personal."

"This isn't really about me, but if it will help you, I'll answer if I can."

"My brother said he met you in Grand Junction, where you were at some psychology conference and he was there for a different conference."

"Yes, I remember."

"But when I ended up at the ER a couple months ago, and you were there, you acted like you'd never met him before."

She reddened a bit. "Did I?"

"Yeah, you shook his hand and said it's nice to meet you."

If possible, her cheeks pinked even further. "I suppose I—"

"Oh my God. You're attracted to him, aren't you?"

"I don't see how that's any of your business."

"I'm not going to lie. I think he has the hots for you. I've told you that before."

"Honestly, I just didn't want to embarrass you or your brother that day."

"So you did remember him?"

"Yes." She let out a sigh and pulled her long blond hair off her neck. Was she getting hot and bothered? "And this part of our session is over, Mr. Steel."

"Understood." But I smiled to myself. I had to get Joe in here for some therapy. Or to get laid. Maybe both.

"You look a lot like him," Dr. Carmichael said. "About the same height, same build. He has a little more silver in his hair, and his nose is straighter."

"Yeah, you know the bullies broke my nose."

"And you have a younger brother?"

"Yep. Ryan. He's known as the most handsome and as having the best personality of the Steel brothers."

"More handsome than the two of you?" She lifted her eyebrows.

I laughed. "Yeah. And I thought we were getting off this subject."

She shook her head as if to clear it. "Of course. I'm sorry. Let's get back to you with Jade. So she wants you to take your relationship public, but you don't want to. Why does she want to?"

"Well, this cop, who I thought was a friend of mine, asked her out."

"So he's no longer your friend?"

"He asked my woman out."

"Talon, he had no idea she was your woman. That's probably why she wants to make the relationship public."

Of course. I knew that. "Why is this so hard for me?"

"Only you can answer that."

"But you're the shrink."

She smiled. Always amazed me how she didn't mind being called a shrink. "I think you've answered it yourself. You feel like she won't love you anymore when she finds out everything you've been through."

"Yeah, but it's more than that though."

"What's that?"

"There are times, Doc, when I want to kill those three bastards. I dream about it."

"I know you do."

"And when I went overseas, I thought that killing enemies would take care of that desire for blood. But it didn't. Those were empty kills. I did it for my country, and I don't regret it, but it didn't kill the demons inside me like I hoped it would."

"No, because those weren't the people who created those demons."

"They were demonic on their own. Trying to kill me and my men."

"I understand that, but try as you might, you can't make them represent something that they don't represent."

"What if I can never control those rages inside me? What if I can never spend the night with Jade? What if I can never control the dreams I have and I wake up with my hands around her neck again?"

"We've already gone through this. I don't think you will."

"I wish I were as sure as you are."

"You will be sure one day, and it probably will be sooner than you think."

"I hope so."

"In the meantime, Talon, don't you think it's okay to make your relationship public?"

"What if she doesn't stay with me after she finds out everything?"

"First of all, I think she probably loves you enough to stay with you through thick and thin. But let's look at the worst-case scenario. What if she doesn't? What if something happens and she breaks off the relationship? What does that have to do with now? You could make the relationship public now, and if the relationship ends, you simply make public the fact that it ended. This isn't rocket science, you know."

"It makes a lot more sense when you say it." Still, I couldn't bear the thought of anything ending between Jade and me.

"Look, I do understand where you're coming from. I really do. But you've come quite a ways already. Yes, there is more work to do, and we will do it, but if your relationship with Jade gives you happiness, gives you pleasure, why not shout it to the world?"

"Again, it makes perfect sense when you say it."

"You don't have to decide right now. Just think about it. Talk to Jade about it. Let her know your concerns."

"She may not understand."

"True, she may not. But there's just as good of a chance that she will."

"What am I going to do about the tattoo?"

"I think you have to be honest with her. You're not going to be able to forbid her to get a tattoo. She's an independent woman, and if she wants a tattoo, she should be able to have one. But if you tell her why that particular tattoo is a problem for you, I'm sure she'll understand."

"We've been through all that before. It's both a problem

and not a problem."

"True. But for you to see the exact tattoo that one of your attackers had on the woman you love is probably not the best thing in the world. I do understand that, Talon, and I know she will too."

"I hope so, Doc."

★ ★ ★ ★

I got home in time to find Marj whipping up a roast pork loin with cumin and lime. I inhaled the smoky aroma. "Smells good." I leaned down and gave Roger a pet.

"Call it therapy," Marj said. "I sent Felicia home. I needed some good old-fashioned kitchen therapy."

"Look, Marj—"

"Don't. I feel horrible about what happened to you, Talon. I can't stop thinking about it. And I know you kept it from me to protect me." She sighed. "Sometimes I think ignorance is bliss."

"Are you sorry we told you?"

She shook her head. "Of course not. I needed to understand, and now so many things make so much more sense." She paused for a moment. "You have to tell Jade."

I shook my head. "I'm not ready to do that."

"Do you love her? I mean truly love her? As in the forever kind of love?"

I let out a sigh. "Marj, you have to understand something. I want to answer that with a resounding 'yes.' I really do. But I have no frame of reference. I've never had a relationship before."

"Talon—"

"Thirty-five fucking years old, and I've never been in a relationship with a woman in my life. And now I meet the most wonderful woman in the world."

"You got that right. Jade's the best."

"So the truth is, I just don't know if this is the forever kind of love."

"Does it feel like a forever kind of love to you?"

"Yes," I said honestly. "But like I said, I don't have a frame—"

"Stop right there. If that's what it feels like to you, that's what it is. And if you want this to last with her, you're going to have to come clean with her. She can help you. She won't judge you. Believe me, she's helped me through some hard times in my life."

I didn't want to belittle what "hard times" my sister might've endured during her college years, but I was pretty sure they weren't nearly as bad as what I'd been through. "I'm afraid."

"That's understandable. But relationships can't exist without honesty. Without trust."

Trust.

Jade had shown me her trust. She had given me her trust without question, when I didn't deserve it.

Could I give her that same gift?

"I will tell her, Marj. But in my own time, in my own way."

"Have it your way." My sister turned back to the counter and began to chop a head of broccoli.

Would I ever see her smile again? Only a few days had passed since we'd told her the truth. It was still very real and new to her. She would get through it. Hell, if we had gotten through it, she certainly could. But Marj's smile—that toothless, innocent smile of my baby sister when I came home from hell—had helped get me through a lot of pain.

"Right now I've got to figure out a way to keep her from getting a tattoo."

"That's another thing I don't understand, Talon. Why do you care so much about the tattoo?"

"You don't understand. That tattoo she wanted to get... that exact image..."

Marj stopped chopping and turned to me. "What?"

"One of those awful guys who kidnapped me. He had that exact tattoo."

Marj dropped her mouth into an O, the knife slipping from her hands and clattering to the floor, just missing her sandaled toe.

I picked up the knife quickly and set it on the counter. "Marj? What's wrong?"

"Did Jade ever tell you where she found that image?"

I nodded. "Yeah, she said she found it in one of Toby's books."

"She did. But that's not where she first saw it."

My blood ran cold. "And where was that?"

"Her mother's new boyfriend had that exact tattoo. On his forearm."

CHAPTER THIRTEEN

Jade

I was changing out of my work clothes when someone pounded on my door.

"Just a minute," I yelled. I threw my red silk scarf, white linen pullover, and black skirt on the bed and hurried into a tank top and a pair of heather-gray sweats.

I walked to the door. "Who is it?" I'd have to talk to Sarah about installing a peephole. Snow Creek was a small town and all, but I was a young woman living alone. I needed to see who was behind my door.

"It's me."

Talon. I opened the door. He was red with rage.

"Oh my God. What's wrong?"

"Your mother's boyfriend. What's his name?"

"Nico. Nico Kostas. Why?"

Talon ran to my sink and turned on the water. "God, I met him. I fucking shook his hand."

The water turned hot, and steam rose from the falling cascade. Talon pumped out some soft soap and scrubbed his hands. They turned red with the heat.

I strode quickly to the sink and turned off the water. "You'll burn yourself. What the hell are you doing?"

"Where is your mother's boyfriend now?" he asked

through clenched teeth.

"I... I don't know. I haven't seen him since the night of my mom's accident. He said he was flying to Des Moines. He hasn't been back."

"God... Goddamn." Talon raked his wet hands through his tousled hair. "So fucking close!"

"Talon, please. Tell me what's going on."

He turned to me, gripping my shoulders. "What color are his eyes, Jade? This Nico guy. Does he have brown eyes?"

"Y-Yes, I think so. I never paid that much attention."

"Neither did I, goddamnit. If only— Damn!"

"Talon, you're scaring me. What the heck is going on?"

"Why didn't you tell me?"

"Tell you what?"

"Tell me where you saw that fucking phoenix tattoo!"

"I did."

"You told me you saw it in one of Toby's books!"

"I did. I didn't—"

"You saw it first on him! You saw it on that fucking psychopath!"

Psychopath? Nico struck me as a little slimy, but I figured he just wasn't my type. "Talon, my mother would not date a psychopath." Of course, I knew so little about my mother. Maybe she would. But Nico, a psychopath?

"Well, she *is*."

I shook my head to clear it. "I don't understand. Please just tell me what—"

He grabbed me and slammed his mouth down on the mine. It was an angry kiss, a punishing kiss. But what was I being punished for this time? For not telling Talon I had seen the tattoo on Nico?

But still I opened to him, let him take from me, let him punish me with his lips and tongue.

He broke the kiss and ripped my tank top off me. "Get on the fucking bed," he gritted out.

"Talon, I—"

"I said get on the bed. Don't make me repeat myself again."

My lips trembled, but I obeyed. Equal parts of fear and arousal coursed through me.

I sat on the edge of my bed, my breasts bare, my nipples hard and longing for his touch. He grabbed my legs and pulled my sweatpants off. Then he ripped my lace panties in half getting them off me.

"Get on your hands and knees," he commanded.

Shivering, I complied.

Slap! His palm came down on my ass.

Slap! Slap! Slap! Three more times, and the sting tingled through me, morphing into pleasure as I cried out.

"Damn it, Jade!" *Slap! Slap! Slap!*

"Talon—"

"Shut the fuck up!"

Slap! Slap! Slap!

I moaned into the comforter, bracing for another smack. But a feathery light touch drifted over me. First over my stinging ass, and then over my back, and then down my thighs.

"This is a pretty red scarf, blue eyes."

My red silk scarf. It had been one of the last gifts from Colin. I'd gotten rid of most of them, but this one had seemed too nice to give away. It added a splash of color to my otherwise mundane lawyer's wardrobe.

"What can we do with this?" Talon asked.

I gulped in silence.

"Turn over onto your back," he said.

I obeyed, my ass still stinging.

Talon was fingering the scarf. "I think I'm going to use this as a blindfold." His voice, though hard and cold, was laced with desire. "I'm going to cover your eyes with this, Jade, and I'm going to do whatever the fuck I want to do to you."

My nipples were so hard. Adrenaline pumped through my veins. I had no idea what he was going to do, and I didn't really care. My pussy gushed fresh juice.

"I'd like to bind your hands, but you don't have any bed posts."

"Of course not. This is a futon."

"Then you'll have to just hold your hands still. And if you move them, I'll punish you. Sit up."

When I did, he secured the scarf over my eyes and tied it in the back. The silk was cool on my eyelids, and I couldn't see a damned thing.

"Lie down, and put your arms flat on the bed, palms down."

I did as he told me.

"Do not move your hands. If you do, you're going to get more spankings."

I imagined my ass was red as a beet at the moment. Although the idea of more spankings didn't repel me.

Nothing happened for a few moments. Talon was lurking around my apartment, his footsteps creaking on the floor. What was he doing? I had no idea, until—

"Oh!"

Something cold touched my nipple. Ice.

"Your skin is so hot, Jade, it's melting right on you." Little rivers of water flowed over my breast, like an icicle thawing over me.

The ice touched my other nipple, and soon the cold water flowed over the mound of my other breast.

"How does that feel, baby?"

It was an utterly new sensation. But pleasurable nonetheless. "Good," I said.

The cold numbness of the ice cube trailed over each nipple once again and then spiraled around my breasts in larger and larger circles. It trailed down my abdomen, dipped into my navel for a scant minute, and then traveled over my vulva and nudged the tip of my clit.

"Oh!" But I didn't move my hands. I locked them flat on the bed.

"Good, good," he moaned. "I'm going to put this ice cube in your hot little pussy now. Don't you dare move your hands."

My thighs quaked as the cold ice cube trickled into my tunnel. "Spread your legs as far as you can, baby. That's right. Now I'm going to suck on your clit while this ice is in your pussy. Don't you dare move your fucking hands."

I trembled all over.

"Yeah, baby, here comes the water. Your hot little pussy is melting the ice." He licked my clit.

I grabbed fistfuls of the comforter, willing myself not to move my hands. I wanted to touch my nipples so badly, to pinch them and play with them. But I was determined.

He sucked my clit between his lips, and the ice cold penetrated through me.

God, he had ice in his mouth, too.

He sucked on me, sucked at my pussy. And soon I grabbed the sheets and plummeted into a climax so deep, so amazing, that I wasn't sure where I was for a moment.

"Yeah, baby, come for me. Come all over my fucking face."

I must've melted all the ice, because then Talon's fingers were in me, pumping me, milking me for every last drop of orgasm.

He sucked on my clit again. "Come for me again. Come."

At his command, I did. My whole body shuddered, and I felt like I was racing to the moon.

"That's it, baby. Come. Come when I tell you to come."

My thighs were still quivering from the coldness. Had anything ever been so good?

Seemingly of their own accord, my fingers trailed to one nipple and started playing with the hard bud.

But Talon noticed. And in the back of my mind, I had known he would.

"I told you not to move your hands." He flipped me over onto my stomach quickly and—

Slap!

"God, baby, your ass is so red, so beautiful."

Slap! And then his tongue, more ice, right over my asshole.

I quivered and groaned, my face smashed into the comforter.

"You like that, baby? You like my icy tongue in your ass?"

"Yes, yes," I mumbled into the comforter.

As the ice melted, the water dribbled from my asshole down onto my swollen pussy lips. I gulped, grasping the quilt again.

"Easy now, baby. I'm going to put this ice cube in your ass."

The coldness ripped me open, and I willed myself to relax. When he breached my ring of muscle, I sucked in a breath.

"Yeah, baby, it's melting so fast."

Soon all I felt was the gush of cool water.

"Talon, God. God..."

"That's right, baby. This is *my* ass." And then his hot tongue soothed the coldness.

He tongued my asshole and then inserted his fingers back into my pussy.

I was going crazy here, and soon I was splintering into a million pieces, climaxing high to the sky.

"Talon, please. I need your cock inside me. Please."

I heard the clicking of his belt buckle, the unzipping of his zipper. And then—

He filled me, completing me.

"God, baby, your pussy feels so good."

"Yes, so good."

"Your sweet ass is so red. Do you like it when I spank you, baby? You like it?"

"Yes," I sobbed into the comforter.

Thrust. Thrust. Thrust.

"I want you to come again for me, baby. I'll take you to the fucking stars."

His words sent me over the edge. I spiraled into nirvana, my whole body trembling, culminating in my pussy. "God, Talon, God."

"That's it, baby. Come. Come all over me."

Thrust. Thrust. Thrust.

With one last groan, Talon pushed into me just as I was coming down from my orgasm, and as I felt every pulse of his cock when he released, I spiraled into the vortex again. Coming, coming, coming.

When he finally pulled out and flopped onto the bed next to me, I flattened and turned on my side to face him. I removed the scarf, and tears flowed from my eyes. For some reason, the sight moved me beyond measure.

"Talon..."

He opened his eyes and turned toward me. "Baby, don't cry."

"Don't worry. They're good tears."

"I didn't hurt you?"

I shook my head. "No, you didn't hurt me. You never could."

"I wish I could be sure of that. I came in here so fucking angry."

"I'm sorry I didn't tell you where I saw the tattoo. I didn't think it was that big of a deal."

He sighed, the agitation within him visibly returning. "You have no idea."

"Talk to me. Tell me what's going on. Tell me what this Nico Kostas means to you."

"He's the fucking devil."

I nearly jerked off the bed. "Why would you say that?"

"I can't get into it right now."

I sat up. "Talon, my mother is dating this person. If he's the devil you say he is, I need to know. I need to keep him away from my mother."

"I thought you didn't care much about your mother."

"She's still my mother. She gave me life. Seeing her lying there, so helpless, I've kind of had a change of heart. I want to see her recover. And if she recovers, I don't want her hanging around with someone who's a bad person."

Talon shook his head. "Blue eyes, you have no idea."

"Then tell me. Please. Just be honest with me. I can take it. I promise you."

"I wish I could, Jade. I'm just not ready yet. But please, keep your mother away from him."

"So far I haven't had to worry about it. After you and I showed up at the hospital the other night, he left. Like I told you, he said he was going to Des Moines, and I haven't seen him since."

Talon cleared his throat. "I'm not surprised."

"Why?"

"I can't get into it. But I will find him, Jade. I will find him. I promise you that."

CHAPTER FOURTEEN

Talon

She didn't push me any further to talk about Nico's tattoo, and for that I was grateful. But still, a look graced her beautiful face—a look that said she wasn't letting this go. I didn't expect her to. I knew her that well at this point.

She sat up and let out a moan.

"Are you okay?" I asked.

She let out a chuckle. "Yeah, my ass is a little sore."

"I'm sorry, blue eyes. You have to let me know if I get too rough. Maybe it's time we talked about a safe word."

"A safe word?"

"Yeah. It's a tool dominants and submissives use. It's a word that means 'stop.'"

"Why not just use the word 'stop?'"

I let out a laugh. "Because sometimes people like to act out fantasies of being assaulted or attacked, and yelling 'stop' is part of the fantasy."

"I can assure you I don't have any fantasies like that."

"All right, then. We'll use stop as your safe word."

"Works for me."

"So why didn't you tell me to stop tonight?"

"Because." She hedged. "Talon, I want to please you. I want to please you more than anything in the world. And clearly you needed this tonight. You needed to spank me for whatever reason. You were angry, and I wanted to help."

"Hurting you is never what I require, blue eyes."

"I know that. If it had gotten to the point where I absolutely hadn't been able to take it, I would've told you to stop. But I can take a lot, Talon, and I want you to take what you need from me."

Had there ever been a more wonderful woman in the world? A woman made just for me? For that's what I believed Jade to be. I was determined to become worthy of her and her love. And of her trust.

"There's something I want to tell you, blue eyes."

She caressed my cheek. "What's that?"

"I don't want you to see this as a weakness."

"Talon, you're about the strongest person I know."

"How can you say that? You've seen me crazy, angry, almost delusional."

"And you come out of it every time."

I paused a moment. Then, I heaved a sigh. "I've been seeing a therapist."

She didn't bat an eye. "Oh?"

"Yes. I have a lot of stuff I have to work out."

"You mean from what happened overseas? Or is there more? There must be more."

She knew me too well. Most people assumed I had post-traumatic stress disorder from my time overseas. Truthfully, my time overseas had been less horrific than the incident in my childhood. "Yes, some other things."

"Can you tell me about it?"

"Not yet, blue eyes. But I will. I promise I will."

God love her, she didn't push. But she did continue

speaking. "Can I tell everyone that I'm in a relationship with you now? I mean, that's kind of where this whole thing started."

Everything at me screamed to tell her no, that I wasn't ready for that. But I had to trudge uphill. I had to step out of my comfort zone. This would be a good start.

"Yes, blue eyes. I would be proud and honored to have everyone know I'm in a relationship with you."

She smiled a gorgeous smile and climbed on top of me, searing my lips with hers. We kissed hungrily until I began to harden underneath her again. She didn't miss a beat. She sank her cunt down on my cock and rode me, slowly this time—slow, sweet love.

"I love you, Talon," she said, playing with her nipples as she rode up and down on my cock. "I love you so much."

"And I love you, Jade." I poured every ounce of love from the depths of my soul into those words, and I hoped she felt it.

We climaxed together, moving in perfect harmony, in perfect synchrony, like two strings of a violin quivering with the same music.

When we both finished, completing each other, she rolled off me and curled into my arms.

"Talon?"

"Yeah?"

"I need to talk to you about something."

"What's that, blue eyes?"

She exhaled. "Colin."

I stiffened. Agitation coursed through my veins. "After that beautiful lovemaking, you bring him up?"

"It's nothing like that, I promise. It's just that, his father has called me a couple times. It seems he's disappeared."

"Good riddance," I said.

"This is serious. He's disappeared, and so has Larry Wade, my boss."

"Well, I can't say the world isn't a better place without both of them, but I don't know anything about it."

"I just want you to be careful," she said. "It's no secret that there's no love lost between you and Colin. People are going to ask questions. That's why Steve Dugan came to see me."

"He hasn't gotten around to me yet."

"He will. I had to tell him the truth, Talon. I told him the last time I saw Colin was that Friday night, when you and your brothers found us together. Remember? He laughed and said he was going to be in court on Monday? And then he didn't show."

"I just figured he thought better of it."

"That's what I figured too, at the time. But looking back, I was just thankful he hadn't shown up. It wasn't like him at all. He had pledged to make trouble, and usually, when Colin sets his mind on something, he sees it through."

"So you think whatever happened to him happened sometime between the time we saw him on Friday and court on Monday."

"That would be my guess. I expected Colin to show up at court."

"You want me to look into it, blue eyes?"

"No. You have enough on your plate right now with your own therapy and running the ranch. I'll figure this out. I'm just glad to know you have nothing to do with it."

"I won't deny I hate the guy, but the last time you saw him was also the last time I saw him."

"And your brothers?"

"Blue eyes, my brothers have way more sense than to get

involved in anything illegal. Trust me, I'm the one *they* worry about. They're both very level-headed."

"I believe that they are, but Colin pushed all their buttons. Even Ryan got agitated at the end."

"True. Not much gets to Ry."

"But Colin did."

True. Colin had. And Ryan would do anything for me. "If it makes you feel any better, I'll talk to my brothers. But I can tell you with ninety-nine point nine percent accuracy that they had nothing to do with him disappearing."

"Okay, good."

"And what's this about your boss missing?"

"Yeah. It's the weirdest thing. He left a little bit early Friday, to take his grandkids somewhere. And then I was almost sure I saw him talking to Nico in the hallway at the hospital around midnight that night. But in a flash they were both gone, so I could have been mistaken. I haven't seen either one of them since."

I stiffened again. Larry Wade. I knew very little about him, other than he'd come to town and been appointed city attorney when the old one retired. But if he was hanging with Nico Kostas... My spine went cold.

Jade went on, "Anyway, the mayor is pissed that nobody can find him. In fact, he made me acting city attorney for the time being."

"That's a good thing, right?"

She let out a laugh. "I'll say. There will be no more bending of ethics with me in charge."

"Well, it was his bending of ethics that got me off with Colin."

"True enough. But Talon, he's a sleaze—" She stopped

abruptly, as if there was something else she wanted to say but thought better of it.

"And?" I pushed.

"And...what?"

"Never mind."

As curious as I was, she hadn't pushed me on things I wasn't ready to talk about, so I would not push her.

Then she jerked upward into a sitting position. "Oh my God."

"What?"

"You don't think Colin's disappearance and Larry's disappearance are related, do you?"

"I don't see why they would be. Colin disappeared way before Larry."

"It's just that...something is so weird about all of this. Why would Larry just fall off the edge of the earth? He had a good thing going as city attorney. Yeah, he's a sleaze ball, but as far as I could tell, he had a great relationship with his grandkids. Why would he leave all of that behind?"

"I don't know, blue eyes. But I can give you the name of a few really good PIs if you want to investigate it."

"I have everything at my disposal at the city attorney's office. I can investigate it myself." She lay back down, snuggling into my arms. "Talon, will you stay with me tonight?"

And I stiffened once more. She was asking me for the one thing I couldn't give her. "Blue eyes, I can't. And you know why."

★ ★ ★ ★

My guts were churning as I gripped the arms of the hunter-green chair. I couldn't stop thinking about Jade's mother's boyfriend, the man named Nico Kostas. I had Googled him when I returned home.

The Internet held precious little about the man, considering he was supposedly a politician.

"You seem a little more agitated than usual today," Dr. Carmichael remarked.

I didn't know where to begin. "Remember the tattoo? The image of a phoenix that Jade wanted to get permanently inked on her body?"

She nodded.

"I found something out last night. She didn't just find the image in a book. She saw it on a person. On a person's forearm."

Dr. Carmichael widened her green eyes. "Whose?"

"Her mother's boyfriend. His name is Nico Kostas, and he's supposedly a senator from Iowa, but he's lying. There's no record of him anywhere." I trembled. "I met him. I shook his motherfucking hand."

"I understand this is difficult for you. But you know, Talon, just because this person had the same tattoo on his forearm as the one you remember doesn't mean he's the same person who abducted and tortured you."

I knew that. I knew with my objective brain that she spoke the truth. But something niggled at the back of my neck. This was related. I could feel it in the marrow of my bones. "Doc, it just all seems so eerie to me. That he would have the same tattoo that I remember on the same part of his body—his left forearm."

"Yes, I can see that it's very eerie," she said. "But still, you have no evidence—"

"Damn it!" My fist came down on the leather of the chair.

"I don't know how to explain it. I just *know*. I know in the depths of my soul that this guy is the guy."

"You say you met him?"

"Yeah, I did. Jade's mom was in a car accident, and he was the driver. He walked away unscathed, but Jade's mother's airbag didn't deploy, and she was badly injured."

"My goodness, will she be okay?"

"They think so. She's unconscious most of the time now, but the prognosis is good."

"Well, that's good at least. Let me ask you, Talon. Did you feel any hint of recognition when you met this man?"

I shook my head. "I wouldn't recognize any of them if I saw them on the street. They were always masked. The only thing I remember about the worst one is that he had that tattoo on his left forearm and he had brown eyes."

"And this Nico, did he have brown eyes?"

I closed my eyes. "I wasn't looking that closely. But I think he did. And Jade thinks he has brown eyes. He has a Mediterranean look, you know, olive skin and black hair. So they were most likely brown."

"Perhaps you should pursue this, Talon," Dr. Carmichael said. "It could be a shot in the dark, but at least it's a shot."

"I have every intention of pursuing it. But the guy seems to have fallen off the face of the earth." And so had Jade's boss. Could there possibly be any relationship between the two?

"I wonder..."

"What?"

"You met him. You told him your name, right?"

"Either I did or Jade did. I can't remember."

"Hmm, I don't know, Talon. It could be a coincidence that he disappeared after meeting you, or it could be that meeting you sent him into hiding."

God. This was all too much for me right now. Was it truly possible that I had found one of my abductors? Only to have him disappear? My mind wasn't ready to deal with this, so I did the only thing I could at the moment. I changed the subject.

"Jade asked me to stay the night with her last night." I gripped those damned hunter-green chair arms.

"And?" Dr. Carmichael said.

"And I couldn't. You know why."

"Did you want to?"

"Of course. More than anything." And that was definitely the truth. I wanted to be with her more than anything. I never wanted to let her out of my sight. I wanted to protect her with everything that I was. But I knew I wasn't ready to do that yet. Before I could protect her, I had to heal myself.

"When do you think you'll be able to spend the night with her?"

"I don't know. What if I never can?"

Dr. Carmichael smiled. "Talon, you will be able to. We will work and get you through this, and one day, you will be able to spend the night with the woman you love."

I hoped with all my heart she was right.

"I'd like to suggest something to talk about for today," she said.

That was fine with me. It saved me from having to figure out something to talk about. "Sure, what do you want to talk about?"

She handed me a piece of paper. "This."

It was a photocopy of a news article from the *Snow Creek Daily*. "Local Hero Comes Home." Damn. But I figured we'd have to talk about this sooner or later. I scanned through the article, my nerves on edge.

★ ★ ★ ★

Local resident and Award of Honor recipient Talon Steel returned home to Snow Creek this past week. Talon entered the Marine Corps as a second lieutenant and quickly gained the rank of first lieutenant and then captain due to his hard work and heroism. He was deployed first to Afghanistan and then to Iraq. He received the Award of Honor from the governor of Colorado for making six death-defying forays into a killing zone to save six American troops. Captain Steel was thirty-two years old at the time of his return. He was granted an honorable discharge.

"Captain Steel is a hero to us all and a great example of a model citizen of Colorado," said the lieutenant governor. "We are proud to have him home to our great state."

★ ★ ★ ★

I stopped reading but glanced at the last line.

Captain Steel made only one comment: "I didn't do it to be a hero."

I let out a sigh. "All right. I figured you'd find this eventually."

"This is amazing. You truly were a hero."

Hero. There was that word again. People loved to throw it in my face, most notably my little brother. I wasn't a hero. I sure as hell didn't feel like one.

"How does this article make you feel, Talon?"

Why not admit the truth? "It makes me feel like a fake, a fraud. I'm no hero."

"I beg to differ. You saved six soldiers. That equals a hero in my eyes. In most other people's eyes as well."

"Let me tell you just how much of a hero I was that day." I clenched the armchair. "I went back in and saved all of those people because I was hoping to get my ass shot off myself."

She didn't bat an eye. "Really? Let's talk about that a little bit. Why were you trying to get killed?"

"Because I couldn't deal with my life. Is that any surprise?"

"No, it's not a surprise, but if you wanted to die so badly, why didn't you just take your life?"

A question I'd pondered more than once. "I don't know. I thought about it, but something stopped me."

"Your will to survive. The human instinct for survival is strong."

I closed my eyes and thought about things, things that happened back during that horrible time. How I'd said those awful words they'd forced me to say just so they wouldn't kill me. My will to survive...

"What are you thinking about?" she asked.

"I never thought I truly wanted to live until recently. The fact that I was held captive, and they threatened to kill me if I didn't do something—something horrible. I always did it. And I hated myself for it."

"But you did it to survive."

I grasped my jawline, my stubble scraping my fingers. "But it doesn't make any sense. I spent most of that time wishing I were dead. So why did I want to survive? Why did I do what they made me do in order to survive?"

"What kind of things did they make you do?"

Admitting this would be torture. But I had determined to get through this. "A lot of times, they made me tell them that

I..." I gulped, swallowing back the nausea that threatened. "I liked what they were doing to me." My knuckles were white with tension as I gripped the armchair.

"I know this is hard for you to say, but it's part of the healing. Anything else?"

"They threatened me, that if I threw up, they'd kill me. Even that first time, when I saw them..."

"Saw them what?"

"My friend Luke Walker. The kid Ryan and I were looking for that first day we went—when I got taken. He was already dead, but they made me watch as they—" My skin got cold and tightened around me, my bowels gurgled, and my stomach threatened to empty.

"It's okay. Breathe. When things get rough, it's always best to go back to the simple essence of life. Breathing."

I breathed in and out. In. Out. In. Out. My body was not relieved of tension, but it was a start. "They told me if I threw up or shit my pants...they..."

The horrors formed in my mind's eye. Luke Walker, thankfully already dead, as his body was cut apart, butchered, the splintering sounds as his bones cracked. His brains and eyeballs as they beat his head in.

"Breathe, Talon."

★ ★ ★ ★

"Don't you dare puke, you little pussy. Watch. Don't close your eyes."

I gagged, swallowing compulsively, trying desperately to ease the nausea that rose in my throat.

"See this? This is what happens when we're done. This is

what will happen to you when we're done with you."

My knees buckled, but because one of the men was holding me up, I didn't fall to the floor. His hands were clamped over my shoulders and upper arms, holding me still, while the other...

At least Luke wasn't screaming.

He was already dead.

No one should have to know what beat-in brains look like. But I would know. For the rest of my short life, I would know. Red sticky jelly, splattering, oozing...

For the rest of my short life, I would know.

★ ★ ★ ★

"They chopped him up. Chopped his arms and legs off." I gulped. "Beat his head in and then chopped it off."

Dr. Carmichael's lips trembled. Just a bit, but I noticed. She was trying to keep her cool. She specialized in childhood trauma, but this could easily have been the worst she'd ever heard. I wasn't about to ask.

"I'm so sorry you had to go through that," she said, clearing her throat.

"Sometimes, I look back, and I just don't get it, Doc. Why, in the face of everything that happened to me—why did I fight so hard to survive?"

CHAPTER FIFTEEN

Jade

I had gotten a phone call from my father at about noon. My mother was finally awake for more than a few seconds at a time, and she wanted to see me. It was Friday, and since I was now the acting city attorney, I gave myself the rest of the day off. I said goodbye to Michelle and David and drove the Mustang I had borrowed from the Steels to Valleycrest Hospital in Grand Junction.

My father was waiting for me in the waiting area outside the ICU. He gave me a quick hug.

"She's looking better, Jade. But still she's not Brooke Bailey yet." He smiled. "We haven't let her look at herself in the mirror."

I couldn't help a small chuckle. "Yes, that would probably devastate her." But maybe now she would learn that looks were not the most important thing in the world.

"She's been asking for you. She also keeps asking for that Nico character."

My blood chilled at his name. The way Talon had reacted, I wanted Nico Kostas to stay far away from my mother. "So he hasn't been back around?" I asked hopefully.

My father shook his head. "Not that I know of. Of course I wouldn't recognize him if I saw him."

"He's a tall and burly Mediterranean type. Good-looking enough."

"And he probably buys her pretty things." My father smiled.

I couldn't help but smile back. "Should I go on in?"

My father nodded. "I know she'll be happy to see you."

I squeezed my father's hand and then left him and walked into the ICU. A nurse was in with my mother, checking her vitals.

"I'm sorry to intrude. Should I come back in a few minutes?"

My mother's cracked lips curved slightly upward. "No, that's my daughter. I want her to stay."

The nurse smiled, finishing up. "You heard the patient. I'm done here anyway. Just a few minutes," she said to me. "Ms. Bailey tires easily."

"I understand." I sat down in the chair next to my mother's bed. "How are you doing, Mother?"

She sighed. "Could be better, of course." Her voice was soft and tired. "Glad to see you though."

"I'm sorry I haven't been able to be here this week."

"Don't worry about that. Your father explained everything. Your work is important, Jade."

Was this my mother I was talking to? My mother who always put Brooke Bailey first and everything else second? My mother was saying my work was important?

"I can probably stay here for the weekend if you want me to. I have to go back for work on Monday. I'm the acting city attorney right now, so it's kind of necessary that I be in the office."

"The acting city attorney? How did that happen?"

I shook my head. "It's a long story, Mom. I'll explain later, when you're stronger."

She sighed. "All right. If you think that's best."

I did a double take. Was this truly Brooke Bailey I was talking to? Never before had she been concerned with what I thought was best. Never before had she been concerned with what anyone else other than she thought was best.

"So do you know what happened to you?"

"An accident. Airbag didn't deploy, evidently."

"That's right," I said. "You're really lucky to be alive."

"Yes, I suppose I am. I guess my modeling days are over, though they've kind of been over for a while."

"Are you in a lot of pain?"

"No. They've got me good and drugged up. I don't want to think about what the shattered knee is going to feel like."

"They'll take good care of you here. They have so far. The doctors saved your life."

"I know that. I just don't understand."

"Understand what?"

"Where is Nico? Is there something people aren't telling me? He didn't...die, did he? Your father kept dodging my questions."

I gulped down a lump that had formed in my throat. I didn't want to lie to my mother, but I also didn't want to jeopardize her health. "Don't worry about Nico. You need to focus on getting better."

She widened her eyes as much as she could. "Jade, your father... He's always had a soft spot for me, no matter what. Even when I came back when you were fifteen, and I wanted to come back into your lives, he was ready to let me, but he chose not to for your sake. Because you were so against it."

"Mom, this is not the kind of discussion to keep your stress level down where it needs to be."

"Jade, please, I have to say this."

I sighed. "All right. Go ahead."

"Your father has always tried to protect me, no matter what. But from you, Jade, from you I know I can get the truth. Now tell me, and do not lie to me. What happened to Nico?"

I drew in a breath and let it out slowly. "Are you sure you want to go there right now?"

She nodded.

"All right. Nico is fine. His airbag functioned just fine, and he got out with hardly a scratch."

"Then why isn't he here?"

"I don't know. I saw him briefly the night of the accident when I came to the hospital to see you. Then he left, said he had to fly to Des Moines, and I never saw him again." Not true. I had seen him talking to someone who I thought was Larry, but there was no need to bring that up.

"That doesn't seem like Nico. He...loves me."

"Of course he loves you, Mother. I'm sure he has a very good reason why he's not here." I didn't believe that for a minute, but I didn't want to upset my mother any more than she already was in her fragile state.

"There's something else I need to talk to you about," she said.

"What's that?"

"I hope you will let me back into your life, Jade. There's nothing like almost dying in an accident to make you realize what's important."

Yeah, there was. Nico. She'd talked about Nico before she got to this. But again, I didn't want to upset her.

"Mother, we can talk about this when you're stronger."

"No, Jade, I want to talk about it now. I was wrong. Wrong about so many things. I brought you into the world, and I should've been a mother first. Instead I chose to be Brooke Bailey, supermodel." She coughed.

"Come on. You're not strong enough to be doing this right now."

"No, please hear me out. I've already told your father how sorry I am. He was my first love, you know."

Yes, I knew the whole story of my mother and father. I didn't think it was any riddle why my father hadn't remarried. My mother was his one and only love. He was a good-looking man, and many women had expressed interest over the years. But he threw his life into his work and into me.

"Dad forgave you a long time ago."

"That's what he told me. Honestly, Jade, I didn't know until now. But what I want more than anything is *your* forgiveness."

I didn't know what to say. Here my mother was, having just begun recovery from an accident that could've easily killed her. I couldn't exactly tell her, "No, I won't forgive you." But I had held on to these feelings of resentment for so long. Talon was going through therapy, trying to heal from his past. Should I do the same thing?

Maybe it was time.

I let out a sigh. "All right, Mother, I forgive you." I tried hard to mean the words.

She closed her eyes. "Thank you. I want to be a part of your life. I hope you'll allow me in."

That was another thing altogether. Did I have room in my life for the woman who'd abandoned me? Who put herself before her only child? I'd have to think long and hard about that. Right now, all I could offer was my forgiveness.

"Mother, you're going to be here for a while. But when you get strong and healthy, we will talk about all of this, okay?"

She closed her eyes again. "All right, Jade. If that's the way you want it. I'll hold you to that."

I took her hand and squeezed it. "I promise we'll talk about all of it. When you're more able to do it. In the meantime, your only job is to focus on getting healthy and strong. Okay? Can you do that for me?"

She nodded slightly, her eyes still closed. "I can do that. For you." She drifted off to sleep.

I squeezed her hand and then went back outside to the waiting area where my father was. "She's sleeping now," I said.

"That's the best thing for her."

"She said you told her that you forgave her."

"I did. Truth is, I forgave her a long time ago."

"I know you did, Dad. Why didn't you tell me that you wanted to give her another chance when she came back ten years ago?"

He shook his head. "I couldn't. You were so full of anger and resentment. You were only fifteen, and my first duty was to you, my daughter."

"If you'd told me..."

"No. I hold no grudge against you, Jade. I made a vow to you when your mother left that I would care for you, that I would be both parents to you, and that you would come first. Your needs would come first."

"Maybe it would've helped me to have a mother when I was fifteen."

"As much as I loved Brooke, she wasn't ready to be mother to a fifteen-year-old girl. It would have made things worse.

And there were no guarantees that she would stick around, no matter what she said. I couldn't take the chance she would do that to you again."

"Yeah, she might've left again," I said.

"Exactly. And that would've hurt you even more. No, I couldn't do it. As much as I wanted to be with Brooke, I couldn't."

I gave my dad a hug. "I'm so sorry, Dad. I'm so sorry you couldn't have the woman you loved because of me."

"You have nothing to be sorry for. You were my focus, Jade. You were and still are everything to me. Sometimes I miss you so much I can't see straight."

"I miss you too. But I'm not that far away. You can always call or text more or come and visit."

"You know I hate phone calls. But I think maybe I will visit more often."

I pulled back from a hug and smiled. "I'd like that."

CHAPTER SIXTEEN

Talon

"The human instinct to survive is strong."
My mind kept flowing back to Dr. Carmichael's words.

"You may have thought you wanted to die during that horrific month you were in captivity, but inside, in the very essence of you, your id—the uncontrolled part of your personality that contains your basic and instinctual drives—you wanted to survive. You wanted to live. And that's why you said those words. To survive."

"But I hated myself every time I said them," I countered.

"Humans often do things they hate to survive. You're hardly the first to do that."

Deep down, even hating my circumstances, had I truly wanted to survive?

"But what about the news article? I went back in to rescue those people, knowing full well I could get my ass shot off."

"Maybe your instinct kicked in again, your id. You thought you were going into it to die, but instinctively you dodged fire and pulled others out. Your soldier training kicked in. It was instinctive."

I scoffed. *"Now you're making me sound like the hero everyone else thinks I am."*

Dr. Carmichael rose from her chair, her eyes serious, her countenance strong and firm. She stood directly in front of me, looking down, her green gaze penetrating mine.

"It's time you realize something. You are a hero. You saved six people that day who couldn't save themselves. And even more, you saved a scared ten-year-old little boy. You saved his life, Talon. When the uphill battle seems unwinnable, when you're ready to throw in the towel, remember that. Remember your strength. You are worth something. And you deserve happiness."

★ ★ ★ ★

Jade had texted me that she went to Grand Junction to visit her mother, who had awoken. After I was done with therapy, I drove out to the orchards and checked in with Axel. Everything looked good, so I went back to the house, prepared for one of Felicia's awesome Friday-night dinners.

But again, Marj was in the kitchen.

"I thought you had cooking class tonight," I said.

"I decided not to go. I'm just not in the right frame of mind for it."

My poor baby sister. Maybe I had given her too big of a cross to bear by telling her my story. She wasn't dealing with it very well.

"I'm making *coq au vin*," she said. "It will be ready in about half an hour."

I tunneled my fingers through my hair. "Look, Marj. I'm really...sorry."

"You're sorry? Talon, you have nothing to be sorry about. I hate that you went through all of that."

"I know you do. But I hate seeing you like this. Sometimes

I wish we hadn't told you."

She wiped a speck of spilled gravy from the counter. "Please, don't feel that way. It's just..."

I understood. She couldn't put it into words. It was that dreaded mixture of pity for me and horror at the entire situation. I'd faced it before from my brothers. I hated it, but I couldn't bring myself to blame my little sister for feeling that way.

"You cook when you're upset."

"It keeps my mind busy, you know? But even so..."

But even so, it still hovered over her. I got it. She had no idea how much I got it.

Time to change the subject. "So Jade's in Grand Junction with her mom tonight."

"Yeah," Marj said. "She texted me. I guess it's good that Brooke woke up."

"Did she tell you that the mayor made her acting city attorney?"

Marj nodded. "Yeah, who can figure that out? How could Larry Wade just up and disappear?"

"He's not the only one who disappeared."

"Who else disappeared?"

"Her ex, Colin. Evidently he hasn't been seen since the Friday night when he insisted on taking Jade to dinner."

Marj dripped her jaw open. "I wonder why Jade hasn't mentioned it to me?"

"I have no idea. Steve Dugan was talking to Jade about it. The jerk asked her out, too."

That got a smile out of my sister. "I bet that didn't go over well with you."

Sometimes I was surprised how well Marj actually knew

me. "Nope. So I told her we could make our relationship public."

Marj smiled, and it almost looked like her real smile. "Really? That's wonderful."

"I hope so. I hope I can be everything she deserves. I'm just not sure sometimes."

"Talon, despite what you may think, you *are* a whole person. You're dealing with this now. All Jade needs is someone who will love her more than anything. If you can do that, you're exactly what she deserves."

"I hope you're right."

"I am. But that's totally weird about Colin."

"I know," I said. "It doesn't look too great that Jade and Joe and Ryan and I were the last ones to see him. But I went home with Jade that night. So she and I can give each other an alibi. I'm more concerned about Joe and Ryan."

"They probably each went home to their own houses."

"Yeah, and then no one probably saw them after that."

"Talon, our brothers had nothing to do with this."

"I know they didn't. But they're going to be questioned—if they haven't been already."

"If they had been questioned, we probably would have heard about it."

She was no doubt right, but still, something gnawed at the back of my neck. "I don't know why, Marjorie, but I feel like something is about to go down. Something big."

CHAPTER SEVENTEEN

Jade

I ended up driving back to Snow Creek. I'd planned to stay the weekend in the city, to spend as much time with my mother as I could, but my father seemed to need to be with her, and I didn't want to intrude on their time together. And that wasn't a lie, but it wasn't the main reason I drove back. I had an uncontrolled urge to be with Talon. I arrived at the ranch house at about eight o'clock. I knocked, and Talon let me in, Roger panting at his heels.

The enticing aroma of garlic and thyme wafted out from the kitchen. I inhaled.

"Marj made *coq au vin*," Talon said. "There's plenty left if you want some."

I hadn't eaten, and at his words, I found that I was famished.

"Thanks. Don't mind if I do."

He went with me in the kitchen and pulled a plate out of the cupboard.

"Go and sit down. I can take care of this." I fixed myself a plate of Marj's masterpiece, warmed it up in the microwave, and poured myself a glass of red wine. "Do you want a glass of wine?" I asked Talon.

He shook his head.

I sat down at the table and gestured to the seat next to me. "Sit with me while I eat."

Between bites, I told Talon about the conversation with my mom.

"How does that make you feel?" he asked.

I couldn't help but smile. "You definitely have been in therapy, haven't you?"

"What do you mean by that?"

"I think that's the first time you've ever asked me how something made me feel."

His face was troubled for a moment. "Jade, I've been selfish."

I swallowed the bite of delicious chicken I'd taken. "What do you mean? Where did that come from?"

"I've been so involved in my own problems, I've been blind to everything around me. And I'm...sorry for that."

"Do you want to tell me? About your therapy?"

He visibly swallowed and shook his head. "I'm not quite ready for that yet. Please be patient with me."

"I will be as patient as it takes. You mean everything to me, Talon. You go at this at your own pace, and just know that I will be here whenever you need me."

"You have no idea how much that means to me."

I smiled. "I think I do."

Talon looked at me, his eyes serious. "You never answered my question."

I finished the last of my plate full of delicious French cuisine and took the last sip of my wine. "What question was that?"

"I asked how the conversation with your mother made you feel."

I smiled. He truly wanted to know. This was a huge leap for him. I had never thought of Talon as selfish, but truly, he had been encased in his own little world, and I still didn't know the exact facts of that world. But I had told him I would be patient with him, and even though I wanted more than anything to know what was going on, I would wait until he was ready to talk to me.

"Honestly? I don't know what to feel. I feel like my emotions have been on a roller coaster, like they've been stretched to their absolute maximum and then snapped back into place. This is a woman who basically abandoned me, who chose her career and her second husband over her small child. But she's still my mother. And she's the only mother I'll ever have. So part of me truly wants to get to know her. But then I feel like she doesn't deserve that."

"Blue eyes, it sounds like you want to punish her."

"Well, what if I do? She certainly deserves it."

"Yes, she does deserve it. She should never have abandoned her child. But by punishing her, who are you hurting?"

"Well, her."

"True. But you're also punishing yourself. Denying yourself your mother."

I couldn't help a small laugh. "Therapy's been good for you, Talon. You've gained a lot of insight."

"Blue eyes..."

"Oh, come on. Don't get testy. This is a good thing. I'm giving you a compliment. And you're right. Punishing my mother will only result in negative feelings for me. I should give her another chance. It's just that, she may end up leaving me again."

"True. She may. But you're a grown woman now, Jade. She

can't hurt you anymore the way she did. At least you'll know you tried. You'll never have to wonder what if."

I'd always known Talon was brilliant, but this new insight amazed me. Whatever therapy was doing for him, I hoped it was helping him as much as he was helping me right now.

"You know what I'd like to do now, blue eyes?"

"What's that?"

"I'd like to take you to my bed."

I wasn't about to argue with that. I stood, rinsed off my plate and glass in the sink, and turned to him. His dark eyes were ablaze with fire. He stalked toward me, like a wolf stalking his prey.

"Remember last time, when I blindfolded you?"

I nodded, trembling.

"Did you like that, blue eyes?"

Still trembling, I nodded again.

"Then I have a big surprise for you." He grabbed me, lifted me in his strong arms, and carried me out of the kitchen, down the hallway, to his bedroom.

He put me down and then sat on his bed. "Undress for me, blue eyes."

This wasn't the first time he'd asked me to undress for him, and I wanted to give him a treat. But as usual, I was wearing a pullover top. My large chest negated button-up blouses, but right now, I would have loved to be able to provocatively unbutton each button at a time, baring just a tiny bit of warm skin, to drive him crazy. All I could do was pull my top over my head. So I did, trying to do it as slowly and provocatively as I could, but within a few seconds the top was off, and I tossed it to the floor. I stood in my bra and my black pencil skirt. I was wearing regular black pumps with no pantyhose. At that moment again, I wished for a front-clasp bra that I could tear open, and my breasts would fall gently of their own accord. But no, it was a back-clasp thirty-four double D, and unclasping it wasn't sexy. But I did it, tossed it to the floor, and my breasts were bare.

He eyed me lasciviously. "God, Jade, you do have the most luscious tits in the universe."

I smiled. Evidently my striptease was having the desired effect, even though I didn't find it particularly provocative.

"Remember those nipple clamps, blue eyes?"

I gulped. He had only used them once before, and they had been such a turn-on. I heated all over, and my pussy started throbbing.

"I think we might be seeing them again tonight," he said. "Along with some other things."

Tingles shot across my skin.

"But first you have to get naked."

I smiled as I kicked my pumps off. Then I slid my stretch pencil skirt over my narrow hips until it was a black puddle around my feet. I kicked it toward my shoes.

I slid my finger inside the waistband of my leopard-spotted thong, getting ready to rid myself of it, when Talon shook his head slightly.

"Leave it on for a minute, blue eyes. Let me just look at you. You're so sexy. So beautiful."

I had never been overly excited about my body. I knew I had great boobs, but most of the time they were more of a pain than a pleasure for me because I was so limited in the clothing I could wear. I had a fairly wide waist and narrow hips, and my legs were nothing special. I'd always thought that Marj—long, lean, and lithe—had the perfect body, even though she was nearly six feet tall. But standing here, nearly naked, my breasts falling gently against my chest and my nipples hardening into brownish-pink knobs, with the man I loved more than life itself looking at me with such longing and desire, I felt like the most beautiful woman in the universe.

"Lie down on the bed, blue eyes," Talon said.

My thong still in place, I obeyed.

"Play with those hard nipples," he commanded.

As if of their own volition, my fingers trailed up my abdomen over the swelling globes of my breasts, to find each nipple. Just one whisper of a touch from my own hand, and they hardened even further. I traced my fingers over them first, a light feathery touch, and then I pinched one. I sighed.

"Yeah," he said. "Just like that. You're so gorgeous. Pinch those nipples for me, blue eyes. Twist them."

When I twisted them, spikes of heat bubbled to my core. I was wet. I could feel it—that feeling when my pussy became the whole world. Nothing like it.

"Keep playing with them, Jade. Get them nice and ripe for me." Talon, still fully clothed, walked over to his dresser and came back a moment later.

In his hands, he held the instruments I remembered. They looked like tiny pairs of pliers, the ends covered in black vinyl.

"I went easy on you last time. We'll see how you do today. You ready?"

I nodded. My nipples were hard and ready. He attached one and then the other, and I sucked in a breath.

"Good?"

I closed my eyes. "Yeah, baby. Good."

"The beauty of these is that they're adjustable. This is what I gave you last time. Are you ready for a little more?"

The pain of the nipple clamps was outweighed by the incredible pleasure coursing through my blood. Squeezing them harder would only help, I was sure.

"Please, baby, give me more."

He adjusted them, and I sucked in a breath. Pain. Such good pain. The sense of immediacy, the pleasure, was unmatched.

"Open your eyes, baby," Talon said. "Open your eyes and look at your ruby-red nipples squeezed in the clamps. Fucking gorgeous."

I obeyed and looked down at my ample breasts, my nipples bound between the black vinyl clamps. And oh my God, my pleasure increased tenfold. I had no idea the visual could be so stimulating.

"Oh my God, Talon. It is beautiful, isn't it?"

His eyes were heavy-lidded and glazed over. "So beautiful, blue eyes. You're so fucking beautiful."

I was ready for him. "I'm wet, Talon. So wet for you. Will you fuck me now? Please?"

He stood before me, a beautiful god, still fully clothed. "Not yet, blue eyes. But I can give you a little bit of relief." He removed my thong and inserted two fingers into my wet cunt.

I snapped around him, spasming, convulsing, milking those two fingers. The orgasm coursed through me, all the way up to my breasts, spiraling around to my nipples that were still clamped and so full of pleasure.

"Talon! Talon! God, so good."

"That's it, baby. Come. Come for me. Come all over my fingers. Show me how much I turn you on."

I continued groaning, finally coming down from my orgasmic high.

When I finally opened my eyes, Talon stood over me, a beautiful blur of brown hair, scorching black eyes, and golden skin, but damn it, he still had clothes on.

"Talon, please, get naked. I need you."

His lips curved up to the left. "In good time, blue eyes."

He walked back to the dresser and came back again with more goodies. Were those...?

"Recognize these?"

They weren't anything I had seen from him before, but I knew what they were. Handcuffs. Two pairs.

"These aren't run-of-the-mill toys either. These are real. Solid steel, the kind the cops use."

Shivers shot through me. What would he do with them? I couldn't wait to find out.

"Grab the bars of the headboard, blue eyes."

It never occurred to me to question his demands. I obeyed, and within seconds, he handcuffed me to the bed.

"Are you doing okay with the clamps?"

I closed my eyes and nodded.

"Verbal," he reminded me.

"Yes."

"Remember your safe word?"

"Yes," I said again.

"Use it if this gets to be too much, all right, baby?"

"Yes," I said for the third time.

He walked back over to the dresser and came back with a red bandanna. "This isn't as soft as your silk scarf from the other night, but it will work." He folded it and tied it over my eyes. "Everything all right, baby?"

I nodded.

"Verbal."

"I'm sorry. Yes. Everything is fine."

"Good, good." His voice was low and soothing. "Now spread those pretty little legs, and we'll see what surprises I have in store for you."

My nipples were burning from the clamps, and all I could think of was how much I wanted his cock inside me.

Talon had other things in mind though. Something hard and cold suddenly entered me.

"Ben wa balls, baby. I want you to hold them inside your pussy, okay?"

"Yes," I said.

"God, you're still so wet. I don't even need to lube these up."

Another ball teased the lips of my pussy and then entered me.

"I want you to rock your hips, baby. Rock those beautiful hips and see what this does for you."

I obeyed, and— "Oh!" A vibration, subtle but very pleasurable.

"Keep those balls inside you, baby. If you feel them falling out, pull your muscles in. I want those balls in there."

"Yes," I said.

"I'm going to push your thighs forward. You're going to feel a little bit of lube on your ass, all right?"

"All right." I trembled. I had learned to love ass play. It was so forbidden, so wrong, yet so right.

Some cool liquid trickled over my hole. Talon's finger breached me, and I let out a soft sigh.

"That's right, baby. That's just me. I'm loosening up your pretty little asshole for you."

I sighed again, reveling in the pleasure.

"Now, just a little more pressure."

"God!" I cried out.

"It's a plug, baby. A reminder that this asshole is mine. Got that?"

"Yes." I bit my lip.

"Just relax." He moved my thighs downward, and the plug pushed into me even more. God, so good.

A few minutes passed, and I lay there, totally at his mercy, my nipples clamped, stinging, burning, aching for more. My hips moving, rocking subtly, letting the balls do their job, my ass full, waiting for more.

I felt him before he thrust into me, his warmth hovering over me.

And then his cock was inside my heat.

"God," he groaned. "Those balls inside you create more fiction. Fucking amazing."

He wasn't kidding. They rolled around inside my cunt, and as he thrust in and out, I had double the pleasure, double the sensation. With every thrust, he nudged the plug in my ass as well, giving me even more sensation. It wasn't long before I was plummeting into another climax.

I spiraled outward and then inward, every feeling, every emotion, every physical sensation, writhing into me, as my man fucked me. Fucked me into oblivion.

He groaned above me, taking me, marking me. Marking every part of me. God help me, I wanted to be marked. Wanted to be his.

Wanted to belong to him in every way I could.

"This is me, baby," he said above me, his deep voice like a smooth red wine. "This is me taking you, possessing you."

His words spurred me on. Yes, possessing me. I wanted

him to possess me. His perspiration dripped on my cheeks as he continued pumping, thrusting, until that last thrust when he went so far inside me I thought he touched my soul.

He groaned his release, and when he finally pulled out, we were both panting. The balls tumbled out of me along with his essence.

We both lay still for a moment, until I felt the clamps release my nipples, the plug come out of my ass. And then he unbound my wrists from the headboard.

Last, he removed the bandanna from my eyes.

Finally I could look upon him, the man I loved more than anything. He was beautiful, covered in a glossy sheen, his hair tousled, the strands around his face wet with perspiration. He looked down upon me, his eyes still fiery and filled with a love I had never seen there before.

I closed my eyes, so relaxed, so at peace, and drifted away.

★ ★ ★ ★

When I woke up, the room was dark, and Talon was nowhere to be found.

Well, of course. He refused to sleep with me. I knew he'd never hurt me, and I wanted desperately to spend the night in the arms of the man I loved.

But I'd told him I would be patient. I'd vowed not to push him. He would come to me when he was ready.

I got up and put on my clothes. It was eleven. I walked stiffly around the house, looking for Talon. I found him in his office, engrossed in something on the computer. I decided to leave him to his work. I walked down the hallway to Marj's room. Under her door was a sliver of light, so I knew she was still up. I knocked softly.

"Yeah? Come on in."

I opened the door. "It's just me."

"Oh. Hey. I didn't know you were here."

"I came over to see Talon."

"He said you were in Grand Junction visiting your mom."

"I was. She woke up. She's doing well, and the prognosis is good."

"So what are you doing here, then?"

I smiled. "I just wanted to see him. Now he's in the office working, and I don't want to disturb him. It's late, and I don't feel like driving back to Snow Creek."

"So stay in your old room. No big deal." Her voice was listless.

I sat down on her bed. "Marj, when are you going to tell me what's going on?"

"It's like I told you before. I can't. I wish I could."

I let out a sigh. "Okay."

"How do you like your new job as acting city attorney?"

What a loaded question that was. "It comes with a little pay hike, so that helps. I just got notice that my student-loan payments are starting soon, so the extra they will take from my paycheck every month will make it a little longer to get that down payment for a car."

"You can drive the Mustang as long as you want to."

"I know. I appreciate it. I just hate sponging off you guys."

She gave a little smile and let out a little laugh. The first laugh I'd heard from Marj in a while.

"Haven't we gotten past that by now, Jade? We have more than we could possibly use, and I'm happy to share it with you."

"I know."

"Seriously, how's it going? With work?" She paused a moment. "With Talon?"

"I think things with Talon are going well. He told me he's in therapy."

Marj widened her eyes. "He did?"

"Yes. To be truthful, I'm glad he is."

"Me too," Marj agreed.

"He asked me to be patient with him. Not to press him for information."

Marj smiled again, this time a little bigger smile. "I guess I'll ask you to be patient with me too. If I could tell you what's going on, Jade, I would."

"All right. I understand. By the way, Talon said we could make our relationship public."

"That's great."

"And as for work, I still don't know what to think. I can't figure out why Larry disappeared. He's been gone for a week now, and no one knows where he is. I'll do some investigating of my own on Monday. See if I can figure out where he went." It freaked me out more than just a little bit, but I couldn't let on to Marj how much. After all, Larry had told me to research the Steels. I still had no idea what information he was looking for. He had been tight-lipped about the whole thing. "Do *you* have any idea why Larry might've disappeared?"

Marj shook her head. "I really hardly know the guy. I mean, I had heard that he had dealings with our family in the past."

"I don't like the guy, to be honest." I sighed. "I mean, he gave me a job, which I needed. But he's a horribly unethical attorney. Last Friday, the last time I saw him"—I wasn't going to mention that I thought I had seen him talking to Nico in the hospital late Friday night—"he was wearing shorts and a Hawaiian shirt, getting ready to take his grandkids somewhere. He was looking creepy. You know the kind—like you wouldn't leave children alone with him?"

Marj visibly shuddered, the look on her face unreadable. "What makes you say that?"

"I don't know. He just looked creepy. And not that there's anything wrong with this, but he was missing a toe on his left foot. That's not what made him creepy though."

Marj's mouth popped open. "Are you serious? On the left foot? Are you sure?"

"Yeah." What I didn't tell her was that I'd dropped my gaze to his foot because I hadn't been able to look into his eyes after I'd asked him about Daphne Steel being his sister. I hadn't told any of the Steels about that yet.

Marj jumped off the bed and pulled me up with her. "Oh my God."

CHAPTER EIGHTEEN

Talon

I finished the accounts I was working on, sent a detailed e-mail to our accountant and financial manager, and even though it was nearing midnight, I decided to see if Ryan was up. I felt like sharing a drink with my little brother.

I wrote him a quick text, and sure enough, he was up. *Sure, come on over,* he texted. My brother always welcomed me.

He met me at the front door, wearing his sleeping pants and a T-shirt. "What you doing up so late, Tal?"

"I could ask you the same thing."

"Not much. Was working on some paperwork."

"Same here."

He walked into his family room, and I followed him. He went behind the bar and pulled up a few bottles. "Peach Street, I assume?"

"That'll do it."

He poured me two fingers of the amber liquid and a glass of wine for himself. He sat down next to me on a barstool.

"So what's going on?"

"Just felt like having a drink with my brother."

"You don't want to talk about anything? Therapy?"

I shook my head. I wasn't even going to ask whether Steve Dugan had been in touch with him and Joe. "I am really looking forward to the time when not everything has to be about me. Tonight I just want to share a drink with my brother. Please, just accept that."

Ryan clinked his glass to mine. "I can accept that, bro."

We talked mainly about the ranch until we heard a frantic knocking at the front door.

Ryan stood. "At this hour?"

My first thought went to Dugan. As far I knew, my brothers hadn't yet been questioned about Colin Morse's disappearance, but why in the world would Steve be coming around after midnight on Friday night?

Ryan returned to the family room with my sister in tow.

"God, Talon," Marj said. "Thank God I found you."

"What's going on?"

"First of all, Jade's still at the house. She's sleeping in her old bedroom tonight."

"Okay. You pounded on the door to tell us that?"

She shook her head. "No. I have something way more important to tell you. I was just talking with Jade, and you know her boss, Larry Wade?"

"Yeah, she doesn't like him much."

"No, she said he's unethical and creepy. And guess what else?"

"What?" Ryan and I asked in unison.

"Jade says he's missing the littlest toe on his left foot."

I let the words sink in for a moment. Larry Wade? Here I thought I might have found one of my abductors in Jade's mother's boyfriend, and another one might be her boss? How in the world had my abductors come so close to the woman I loved? I wasn't protecting her very well.

Rage boiled within me.

Ryan sensed my fury. He placed his hand on my forearm. "Talon, a lot of people are probably missing a toe."

"A lot of people here in Snow Creek?" I stood, agitated. "It just seems too coincidental, doesn't it?" My nerves were on edge. My heart beat rapidly, the fight-or-flight instinct kicking in. I wanted to track down Larry Wade, question him, and then beat the life right out of him. "Jade's in her own room?"

Marj nodded. "Talon, don't bother her. She's sleeping, and she's just been through a lot with her mom—"

I stopped listening, striding away swiftly, out the door and back up the path to the main ranch house. When I walked in the back way, I ran through the kitchen and down the hallway to Jade's room. I opened the door without knocking.

"Jade!" I yelled.

She sat up on the bed abruptly, her eyes full of sleep. "What? What is it?"

"It's me," I said. "I need you to wake up. I need you to wake up right now."

"Talon, my God, what's wrong?"

"I need you to tell me everything you know about Larry Wade."

She yawned, rubbing eyes. "Right now? You know what I think of him. He's a sleaze, and he's unethical. What else is there to know?"

"He's missing the pinky toe on his left foot, right?"

She nodded. "How did you know that?"

"Marj just told me. And I want to know why *you* didn't."

She blinked her eyes a few times. "Why *I* didn't? Why would I? It's not really anything to talk about. It doesn't really come up in conversation. So he's missing a toe. Who cares? Why do you care?"

"Suffice it to say that I do care. That little fact is important to me."

"Why?"

"You said you'd be patient with me, Jade. I'm asking for patience now. I'm not ready to tell you why that's important. But I need you to tell me, right now, everything you know about your boss."

She yawned again and then took a drink of water from the glass on her nightstand. "This is obviously very important to you, Talon. So we can talk." She turned on the lamp on her nightstand and then squinted against the light. "I don't know much about him, but I do plan to do some investigating when I get into the office Monday. But in the meantime, there *is* something I know about Larry. It hasn't been confirmed, but I'm pretty sure he's your half-uncle."

CHAPTER NINETEEN

Jade

Talon's eyes widened. "What the fuck?"

Quickly I told him the story about the birth certificates I'd found for both his mom and Larry. About how the name on Daphne's birth certificate had been changed from Wade to Warren. And how someone had to have had big-time access to make those changes.

"That can't be true," Talon said. "And if it is..." His eyes were far away, and a mixture of rage and sadness laced them.

"If it is, what?" I asked.

"You say you got a creepy vibe from him, right?"

"Yeah. I suppose that could just be because he's such an unethical attorney, though."

"No, I trust your judgment, Jade. If you say he's creepy, the guy's a creep."

"Like I said, I don't really know that much about him. I plan to remedy that on Monday."

"Goddamnit." Talon stood, raked his fingers through his tousled hair, and paced around my room. "Goddamnit all to hell."

"Talon, you're freaking me out. What's going on?"

He didn't respond, just kept pacing, and then left my room. Since I didn't have any clothes here, I was wearing my pullover top and my underwear as pajamas. I didn't want to walk around the house that way, so I went next door to Marj's room—she wasn't there—and grabbed one of her robes.

Then I left in search of Talon. He was back in the office, sitting at his computer.

"Where's Marj?" I asked.

"Over at Ryan's, last I saw her."

Why the hell was Marj at Ryan's? But I didn't ask. Talon was clearly on a mission of some sort. He was focused on his computer screen.

"What are you doing?" I asked.

"I'm going to find out who the hell Larry Wade is."

"Why don't you wait until Monday? I have all the state databases at my disposal at work. You won't be able to find anything or do anything more than a Google search from here."

"Not true. I have my ways."

"Talon, it's the middle of the night."

He was clearly disturbed, raking his fingers through his hair constantly. "I don't care. You know I don't sleep much anyway. I've got to find out more about him and about that boyfriend of your mother's."

"Nico?"

"Yeah. Has he come back to see your mom yet?"

I shook my head. He hadn't, and for the life of me I didn't understand why. My mother had been fighting for her life for the last couple of weeks, and her boyfriend had up and disappeared. I didn't get it.

"Do you want me to help you?" I yawned.

He shook his head. "No, go back to sleep, baby. I'm sorry I woke you."

I smiled. I didn't know what was bothering Talon, but the

fact that he said he was sorry that he woke me meant the world to me. Whatever was going on in his head, therapy was helping. It might be that this rampage about finding out about Larry and Nico was just as therapeutic in its own way. I didn't know, and Marj wouldn't tell me. I just had to have faith that Talon would tell me eventually—when he was ready.

I walked over to him where he sat behind his desk and gave him a kiss on the top of his head. "Okay. I'm going to go back to bed. I love you."

$$\star \;\; \star \;\; \star \;\; \star$$

I woke from a sound sleep. My phone was buzzing on the night table. It took me a moment to adjust to my bearings. Light streamed through my window. It was morning—seven a.m. to be exact. Who would call me at seven on a Saturday?

I grabbed my phone—my father.

My heart jumped. Something must've happened with my mom. My skin chilled as I answered the call.

"Dad?"

"Yeah, sweetie, it's me."

"Are you okay? Is Mom okay?"

"Your mother's fine. She woke up early this morning and asked for me. She and I had a very interesting talk."

"Oh?" I was filled with relief that my mother was okay. Strange, I had never cared before about her well-being. Funny how now that I had almost lost her, I desperately didn't want to. "What about?"

"This boyfriend of hers, this Nico Kostas."

A chill ran through me. Talon was also interested in Nico, and I didn't know why. "Did he come back?"

"No. He hasn't been back at all. Your mother is beside herself."

"I'm really sorry she's upset, Dad. But honestly? Something in my intuition tells me it's best that he stays away."

"I have to agree with you, Jade, and I've never even met the man. Something that your mother told me this morning has me very concerned."

"About what?"

"We were talking about him—this Nico—and your mother made a comment about a life insurance policy."

"Yeah?"

"She said that Nico would've been a very rich man if she hadn't survived the accident."

My blood ran cold. I knew where this was going. "Oh my God..."

"Yeah. Evidently your mother had just taken out a one-million-dollar term life insurance policy and had named Nico Kostas as the beneficiary."

"Why would she do that? As far as I know, she's broke."

"Which is maybe why Nico wanted to get rid of her. Your mother's tastes are extravagant, as you and I both know. Maybe Nico got tired of footing the bill. Maybe he got tired of her."

"My God, have you called the cops?"

"Yes, I have. They're coming over to talk to me and to your mother. I'd like you to be here if you can."

"Absolutely. I'm at the ranch right now. I'll shower quickly and be on my way."

"Great. I'll see you soon."

I ended the call.

Could Nico be a killer? I shuddered. Why in God's name had I wanted that tattoo so badly? And it had upset Talon so much. I had already decided not to get that particular image because it upset Talon. Now I wasn't sure I could get *any* phoenix image. All it would do is remind me of the person who might've tried to kill my mother. Why hadn't I thought of it sooner? Nico's airbag had functioned just fine. He had escaped with hardly a scratch. But for my mother's not to deploy? Here she was suffering broken bones, multiple lacerations all over her face and body, and a severe concussion.

That motherfucker.

I stripped off my pullover and underwear and got into the shower. The heat of the water soothed my aching muscles but did nothing to calm the images flowing through my mind like a theatrical trailer. I let out a sigh and leaned my head back into the water to wet my hair. Then I squeezed some shampoo into my palm, rubbed my hands together, and began to wash my hair.

"Want some help with that?"

I nearly jumped out of my skin. Talon stood in the bathroom, his image a blur through the glass shower door awash with rivulets of water.

"You startled me," I said.

"I'm sorry."

I smiled. A little Talon therapy might help me right now. "What are you waiting for? You offered to help."

His feet were bare, but he was still wearing his jeans and shirt. He stripped them off quickly and came into the shower with me.

"Have you been up all night?" I asked.

He nodded, taking over my hair washing. His strong hands were heaven on my scalp, kneading away the tension in knots.

"That feels good," I said. "Did you find out anything?

About Larry?"

"A little. I managed to confirm that the bastard is my half uncle. Son of a bitch."

"Well, just because he's your half uncle doesn't mean anything really," I said.

"Shh. The last thing I want to think about is that asshole Wade when I've got a naked, beautiful, and wet woman sliding against me."

I let out a soft moan. I couldn't agree more. He continued to massage my scalp, his able hands relaxing me, taking me away from the place I was stuck in. Yes, in a few minutes I'd be leaving for Grand Junction to talk to the cops about my mother's possible attempted murder. But right now, Talon was my world.

"Lean back, baby, and let me rinse you."

I did, and his strong hands pulled the lather through to my ends. I imagined it twirling in soapy bubbles down the drain. My eyes closed, I inhaled the comforting steam, the sweet scent of the coconut shampoo. I sighed again and then jumped as his lips clamped onto one of my nipples.

I opened my eyes. He was leaning down, sucking my hard nub. I smoothed his tousled hair, now half-wet. "Let's switch places, baby," I said. "You can nibble on me while I wash your hair."

He groaned his agreement as we moved so the shower was pelting him, and his head was right at the level where I could shampoo him.

"Are you sure you're comfy?" I asked.

He nodded against my breast. I shampooed his beautiful hair and then urged him upward so he could rinse it off, though I whimpered at the loss of his mouth on my nipple. We soaked each other and rubbed together to wash our bodies, and then he picked me up in his arms and set me down upon his beautiful hard cock.

Our bodies slid together, wet and soapy. I leaned down and took his lips with mine. We devoured each other, kissing hungrily, softly moaning, as he lifted my ass slightly and then set me down upon his cock once again.

It didn't take long for my orgasm to build. Such sweet release, and oh, how I needed sweet release at that moment. We spiraled out of control, he and I together, as my orgasm pushed him over the edge.

He broke the kiss with a loud smack, panting in my ear. "Yes, baby, I'm coming. I'm coming with you, baby."

Sated, I slid down his body. We rinsed each other off, and then I turned off the water.

I handed him a towel, and as he stood drying his hair and then his body, I said, "That was wonderful, Talon. You have no idea how much I needed that."

"Baby, I always need you," he said.

"I always need you too. It's just that I got a phone call from my dad this morning."

"Shit, I'm sorry, blue eyes. Is your mother okay?"

"She's fine. Don't worry about that. It's just..."

"What?"

"It's about my mother's boyfriend, Nico Kostas."

Talon visibly tensed before me, the striations in his muscles stark. "Yeah? What about him?"

"It seems that my mother had taken out an insurance policy on her life right before the accident. A million-dollar policy, and Nico was the beneficiary."

He stood stock still, his eyes glazing over.

"Talon?"

"I'm telling you, blue eyes, that man is bad news. I mean it."

"I'm beginning to believe that as well. And Talon? I'm so sorry about the tattoo thing. I just really liked a particular image, but trust me, I'm not getting a phoenix on my body ever. It will always remind me of the man who may have tried to kill my mother."

"I'll see that bastard in hell." Talon threaded his fingers through his wet hair.

He was outraged. I could see it in his demeanor, his eyes, the way he was holding himself. He was ready to strike. But why? He hadn't even met my mother, and he knew she and I were not close.

"Well, we don't know for sure yet."

He hung his towel on the rack. "I do, blue eyes. I know for sure."

CHAPTER TWENTY

Talon

I was nervous as hell driving Jade into Grand Junction to see her dad and talk to the cops. I was going to meet her father. The man who raised her. The man she loved more than anyone. Well, next to me, I hoped.

Believe it or not, that was bothering me more than dealing with this Nico character. If he was who I thought he was, I had no doubt he had tampered with the passenger airbag and tried to kill Jade's mother for the money. If he was who I thought he was... Well, there was no limit to what he would do for his own amusement, let alone financial gain.

He was already guilty in my eyes—not only of abducting and raping me and killing Luke Walker and those other children, but also of attempting to kill Jade's mother. All I needed to do was prove it. Of course, that was way easier said than done.

What made people so evil?

It was the first time I'd asked myself that question. I had really never before thought of those three men as human. Instead, they were the embodiment of evil. Now I might've identified two of them. They were men. Just men. Men I could pummel into next week, kill with my bare hands.

Simply men.

How did men turn into evil demons?

Jade was quiet during the ride, and I didn't engage her. She knew by now that I didn't have the gift of gab, and I was just as happy to be left to my own thoughts during the drive. Thanks to Jade's strong coffee, I was awake. Awake and alone with my thoughts.

I dropped Jade off and then drove around a while, looking for a parking spot, finally deciding to use the valet service. It was Saturday, after all, and many people were here visiting, no doubt.

I signed in as a visitor and made my way up to the waiting area outside the ICU.

My nerves jumped when I walked into the area. Two cops were there, and Jade was already talking to them. Beside her stood a man about six feet tall with the same golden-brown hair I was used to seeing on the woman I loved. He was a nice-looking man, his skin tan, showing wrinkles around his eyes. Jade said he was in construction. He'd probably worked outside most of his life. He looked tired. And not just tired in that he had worked hard all his life. Tired and worried. Worried about someone he loved. Jade's mother, I assumed.

I was going to have to meet her father—the father of the woman I loved. Here I was, thirty-five years old, and I had never met a woman's father before.

Jade motioned me over, smiling. "There you are. Talon, this is my father, Brian Roberts. Dad, this is Talon Steel."

Jade's dad stuck out his hand. "Good to meet you. I've heard a lot about you."

The back of my neck chilled. Jade had seen some of my darker moments, but surely she hadn't shared those with her father. "Nice to meet you too, sir," I said.

Was that right? Did you call a woman's father "sir"?

"Please, call me Brian."

"All right." I attempted a smile. "How's your mom doing, Jade?"

"She's good. They're finally moving her out of ICU today."

"That's great, baby." Then I snapped my head over to Brian. I had just called his daughter baby. But it didn't seem to faze him. Thank God.

"Oh, I'm sorry," Jade said. "This is Officer Shapley and Officer Duke. Talon Steel, my boyfriend."

Boyfriend.

Never had a word imbued me with such warmth. And still, it was woefully deficient. For if I was Jade's boyfriend, that made her my girlfriend—and "girlfriend" was such an inadequate term for what Jade was to me.

"Nice to meet you, sir," the one called Shapley said.

"I didn't mean to interrupt. I can go sit down over there while the officers ask their questions," I said to Jade.

"No, I wish you'd stay. Is that all right with you two, and with you, Dad?"

"It's fine with me, sweetie," Brian Roberts said. "I guess it's really up to the officers here."

"It's fine," Shapley said. "This is just preliminary questioning anyway."

"So do you two think there's enough to warrant an investigation here?" Brian asked.

Shapley, obviously the mouthpiece of the two, replied, "Yes. We're definitely going to take a look at the vehicle. See if we can determine whether the airbag was tampered with. The only problem is that the vehicle has already been repaired. But we'll have our experts take a look."

Jade's face fell. "Why was it repaired?"

"Ms. Roberts," Shapley said, "no one had any reason to think there was any foul play. Mr. Kostas had the vehicle towed from the scene and repaired."

"Mr. Kostas seems to be nowhere to be found."

Shapley nodded. "True enough, and that is also something of a concern."

"He's a senator, for God's sake," Jade said. "He can't just disappear."

"No," I said, my voice low. "He's not."

Jade turned to me, her steely eyes wide. "What?"

"I'm sorry. I forgot to tell you. I did some research on him. I should have mentioned it." I sighed. How could I tell her I'd been side-tracked because of what I'd become convinced he was? I couldn't, at least not in front of all these people

"He's right, ma'am," Shapely said. "He's not a United States senator or an Iowa state senator."

"But why would my mother say..." Jade bit her lip. "I guess she never thought to question him."

"Brooke believes anything someone says if she's getting attention and gifts," Brian said.

"It's certainly easy enough to check out," Jade said, "but that might not have occurred to my mother. She did tend to let men walk all over her."

"To be honest," Shapley said, "Nico Kostas might not even be his real name. But we're definitely going to look into this. That is, if we can find evidence that the airbag was tampered with."

"You've just got to find it, please," Jade begged. "I mean, why would he have disappeared? He supposedly cared about my mother, and now he's just gone. Sounds like someone on the run to me."

"Yes," Shapley said, "it's definitely suspicious. We'll be in touch. Here's my card." Shapley handed one to each of us.

"Thank you for your time, Officers," Brian said.

The two men nodded and walked away.

"I can't believe it," Jade said.

I put my arm around her. "What?"

"The jerk is a liar, and he tried to kill my mother. He's probably going to get away with it. Now that the car's been repaired, there won't be any evidence of his tampering."

"We don't know if that's what happened," Brian said.

I kept my lips closed. That was what had happened all right. Somehow, in the recesses of my bones, I knew. Just like I knew that Larry Wade, my esteemed half uncle, had raped me when I was a child. So had this Nico character. And now he had tried to kill Jade's mother.

Neither of them were going to get away with it.

★ ★ ★ ★

Under the guise of needing to make a few business calls and run some errands, I left the waiting area. Jade was safe with her father, and she needed to be near her mother.

I did make some phone calls, but they had nothing to do with my business. Within ten minutes, I had the name of the body shop where Nico Kostas had taken his vehicle.

I drove over there and asked to speak to the person who handled the car. I was asked to sit until a man called Shem was available.

I thumbed through a *Popular Mechanics* issue from three years ago.

"Mr. Steel?"

I looked up. A young man, tall and thin, grease under his fingernails, his blond hair pulled back in a ponytail, stood before me.

"I'm Shem."

I stood and held out my hand.

He shook his head. "Don't want to get you greasy. What can I do for you?"

"I'm interested in a car that was brought in about two weeks ago. The owner is Nico Kostas."

"Yes, sir, I remember. It was a wreck. He's lucky he got out of it alive."

"Well, airbags are amazing things. Are you aware that he had a passenger?"

"Oh, yeah. Her blood was everywhere. Airbag didn't deploy, I heard."

"Yes, that's what happened." I looked around. "I understand you still have the car."

"Yeppers, got it done. It was damn near a total loss. The only thing that kept it from being totaled was that the car has so much value."

"I have reason to believe the airbag might have been tampered with, and that's why it didn't deploy. I'd like to take a look at the car, if you don't mind."

"You a cop?"

"No, just a friend of the family of the woman who was injured. She's lucky to be alive."

Shem spit on the ground. "I'll say. That car was sure wrecked. And no airbag?" He whistled. "She's damned lucky for sure."

"About the car? May I see it?"

"Sir, it's not your car. I can't release it to anyone but the owner."

"Has the owner been in to claim it?"

"No, sir, he hasn't. Damnedest thing. We've called him every day twice a day for the last week. No one can get hold of him."

Shocking. "Listen, I'd be happy to make it worth your while if you let me have a look at the vehicle. Even more if you let me bring an expert to look at it."

"Sorry, sir. Without a cop, without a warrant, I can't do it."

I pulled two Benjis out of my wallet. "How about now?"

He pocketed them. "Meet me here at seven. Sharp."

I nodded. "Thank you." I left.

I guessed we'd be staying in the city for the night. At least I would be.

I picked up some takeout from a local place and drove back to the hospital. Jade and her dad were happy to have some decent food.

"I'd like to take you to dinner," Brian said. "Get to know you a little better."

My neck chilled. Get to know him a little better? Shit. Talk about a scary thing. So I made excuses. I hoped Jade would understand.

"I'd appreciate that, but I can't. While I was making my business calls, something came up at the orchard, and I need to get back. Baby, go ahead and stay here. Take a cab home if you want. Or spend the night here with your father, and you can see your mom in the morning."

It was a coward's way out. But I couldn't stomach the thought of sitting here in the hospital for the next six hours trying to make small talk with Jade's father. I had to stay until seven, to meet Shem over at the body shop. What would I do in the meantime? I could go back to the ranch and then drive back this evening. Better yet? I'd find a so-called expert to take a look at the car and make it worth his while to come back with me at seven sharp.

CHAPTER TWENTY-ONE

Jade

Getting my mother settled in a normal hospital room was good for my spirits. I wished Talon could have stayed. I so wanted them to meet. But perhaps it was best that he hadn't. I could tell being around my father made him nervous. I wasn't sure why. My dad was the easiest person in the world to get along with. But like Talon had said, he'd never met a girlfriend's father before.

Girlfriend.

The word sounded so juvenile, but it would have to do for now.

My mom was more alert than I'd seen her in a while. The move out of ICU was definitely doing her good. I desperately wanted to ask some questions, but I didn't want to upset her.

"Is there anything I can get you, Mom?"

"No, no. I'm just so glad to be out of that sterile environment."

I smiled. "You're looking so much better. Your face is healing nicely."

"But there will be scars."

I wasn't about to sugarcoat things anymore. She was out of danger. "Yes, there will be scars. But you know? Scars aren't necessarily a bad thing. Scars show that you've been through life. That you went through hell and came back kicking. Scars are a good thing."

"I made my living on my beauty, Jade. I was still a bankable model. Sure, I wasn't making the kind of money I did when I was young, but I was doing okay. I was living check to check, but I was at least making something."

"Who says it's over?"

"Darling, look at me."

"I am looking at you, Mom. I see a strong and beautiful woman whose life is not nearly over. So stop talking like it is."

"No. I've taken everything for granted. I took for granted that I would always be beautiful, and then I started to get older. I started to get laugh lines around my eyes, a few age spots here and there. Nothing good makeup couldn't cover. But now? I have scars from all these lacerations on my face. I'm not sure my eye will ever look normal again."

"Mom—"

"No, let me finish. I always took it for granted. And not just my looks, but people. You, your father. And now Nico."

My hackles rose. Why did she have to mention that jerk? I couldn't tell her that we thought he might've tried to have her killed to collect insurance money. But maybe I could find out why she had taken out the policy in the first place.

"Mom, speaking of Nico, tell me about this insurance policy you took out."

"You mean the life insurance policy?"

"Yeah. If you were going to take out a life insurance policy, wouldn't it make more sense for you to designate your next of kin as beneficiary?"

"You mean you think *you* should have been the beneficiary?"

Crap. I hadn't meant for that to sound the way it sounded. "No, that's not what I mean. I mean, yeah, it's what I mean, but I'm not after any money from you. But why would you name a boyfriend? He wasn't even your fiancé."

"I figured we'd be married eventually."

"I didn't know you were planning to marry again."

She sighed. "For a long time I never thought I would. After that idiot Neal Harmon stole all my money, and then when your father refused to take me back after that. But Nico was different."

"Really? How was he different?"

"He wasn't after my money. After all, I didn't have any. At least not much, anyway."

"Dad was never after money."

"Oh, I know that. But he didn't want me."

"That was ten years ago. What made you decide that Nico might be worth marrying?"

"He was very good to me. He bought me presents, flowers. He made me feel like I was important to him."

"So you decided to take out an insurance policy and named him as beneficiary because he gave you flowers?" I shook my head.

"Actually, the policy was his idea."

Why was I not surprised? "Why would that be his idea? Is there something you're not telling me? Is your health bad?"

"Of course not, silly. If my health were bad, I wouldn't have been able to get the policy in the first place."

She had me there. Frankly, there was only one reason why Nico would've wanted to take out the insurance policy on my mother—so that he could eventually benefit from it. How could I get her to see that? And in her fragile state, did I even want to?

"Why do you think he made that suggestion? I mean, to take out the policy and make him the beneficiary."

"Well, it was his idea to take out the policy because I'm not getting any younger, so it was a good idea to get life insurance now while there were no issues."

"Okay, that actually makes sense. But no one is depending on you, Mom. Dad and I are self-supporting. When there's no one depending on you, there's no reason to take out insurance on your life."

"Well, it made sense to me. I could get the policy now, and it's amazing how cheap term life is from some companies."

"So you decided to get the policy, and he wanted you to make him the beneficiary?"

She shook her head. "Oh, no, that was my idea."

I arched my eyebrows. *Her idea?* "Yes. He suggested you, Jade. Or your father."

"Then why didn't you choose one of us?"

"I did. I chose you. But then I started thinking that the one rock in my life for the last several months had been Nico."

"The last several months? You named a man your beneficiary when you'd only known him a few months? Not even a year?"

"Well, yes. After I chose you, Nico and I talked about the future. He told me he loved me and that he planned for us to live our lives together, and that maybe, since we were going to be married anyway, it might make more sense to make him the beneficiary. Then we wouldn't have to change it later."

"A-ha. So it *was* his idea after all."

"Oh, no. It was my decision."

And once again, my mother had been played by a man. It

wasn't bad enough that her second husband had sucked her dry of all of her life savings. Now this lying jerk had come to suck the life out of her, literally. But I couldn't press it right now. She was clearly getting tired.

"All right. I understand." I didn't, but what good would it do to let her know that? "I think we've talked enough. You need some rest."

She closed her eyes and sighed. "I'm so sorry, Jade. For everything. When Nico comes back, he'll explain it all to you."

When Nico comes back. My poor mother. Still as naïve as the day she was born.

"I'm sure he will. Don't worry about it, Mom. Right now, all you have to worry about is getting rest so you can heal properly."

When she had drifted off to sleep, I went back out to the waiting area and told my father about our conversation.

"He's a slippery fellow, that Nico, huh?" my father said.

"He seems to be. I wish she could see him for what he is."

"When he doesn't come back, she'll have no choice but to see it."

"I just don't understand."

"Well, your mother has two faults. The first one is that she is as vain as they come."

I let out a laugh. "Really? Hadn't noticed that."

"Second one is that she has a hard time seeing people for who they really are. It happened with that second husband of hers, and now it's clearly happening with this Nico. You see, they both showered her with affection, compliments, gifts, and she falls for it every time. That's why she and I never worked."

"What do you mean?"

"Well, there's no doubt Brooke is beautiful. She was a

knockout when I met her, Jade. Amazing. But I saw beneath her looks. I knew she wasn't perfect, and I loved her anyway. I never made her flaws any secret. But she didn't want to be a real person in my eyes. She wanted to be a princess, a beautiful woman who had no flaws—she wanted to be Brooke Bailey, supermodel—and that's how she wanted me to feel about her."

"But you loved her."

"I did. I loved her. Flaws and all. But she couldn't accept that I saw her flaws."

"Still, I feel bad that you couldn't be with the woman you loved, especially when she wanted you back."

"We've been over that before, sweetie. You were my priority then. You're still my priority now. See? Your mother had her priorities all screwed up. Clearly, she still does."

"She did tell me she wanted to try again with me. And she admitted she had taken a lot of things for granted in her life."

My father nodded. "It's all a step in the right direction, that's for sure. A brush with death has a way of making people see what they've previously been blind to."

"If only she could see Nico for who he really is."

"She will, sweetie. Eventually. But she has to figure that out for herself. Neither you nor I will be able to convince her of it."

I sighed. As usual, my father was right. The man had common sense to a fault.

"You know, I wish you could've known your mother when she was younger. She was so full of life. She wanted the world on a platter, and she thought she had it for a while. But fame and fortune are fleeting things, Jade. What's important is people. The people who love us, who need us, who make us feel emotion. That's what's important in life."

My heart swelled. My father had never been a rich man, but he surely was rich in the area of wisdom. I reached over to pat his hand, but before I could, my cell phone buzzed.

"Excuse me." I grabbed my phone out of my purse.

Shit. It was Ted Morse again.

CHAPTER TWENTY-TWO

Talon

So here I was, again, gripping the arms of the green recliner in Dr. Carmichael's office.

Since I had to stay in Grand Junction until seven p.m. anyway, to meet Shem back over at the body shop, I figured I might as well do something constructive. Dr. Carmichael had been amenable to meeting me on weekends in the past, so I'd given her a quick call. She agreed to meet me for an impromptu session.

"What do you want to talk about today, Talon?"

I shook my head. "Hell if I know."

"Have you thought about what we talked about last time? About why you wanted to survive even when you thought you didn't want to?"

"Not really. I mean, clearly I wanted to survive. I did everything they made me do in order to survive. Even though most of the time I wished I were dead."

"There's a big difference between wishing you were dead and actually being dead. I know that doesn't make sense, but the subconscious understands it."

I let out a shaky breath. "I'm glad. I mean...I'm glad I didn't die."

She smiled. "I know you are. I'm glad you didn't too. You

will get through this. You've come so far already. I'm amazed at your progress."

She paused, and I had no idea what to say to that. *Thank you?* That seemed trite. I desperately hoped she'd start speaking again.

She did.

"So you said on the phone you think you've identified two of your attackers now."

"Yeah. I can't be sure, but things sure seem to add up."

"And both those men have disappeared?"

"Yep. And get this. One of them is my half uncle."

"What?" She raised her brows.

"Yeah. Jade's boss, the sleazebag district attorney. Larry Wade. Jade did some investigation, and I was able to confirm it. He and my mother had the same father. It was covered up years ago, and I can't figure out why."

"That is odd."

I shook my head. "I've been over and over it in my mind, Doc. The only thing I can come up with is that my father and mother somehow managed to cover up our relationship with Larry because they knew what kind of man he was."

"It's possible."

"But if they knew what kind of man he was, maybe they knew..." I couldn't bring myself to say the words. Had my mother and father actually known the identity of one of my attackers? And had they let him off the hook? No, that couldn't have happened.

"Are you suggesting that they knew he was one of the men who kidnapped you?"

"I don't know. But why else would they want to cover up the relationship to him?"

"We can only speculate, Talon. Both of your parents are dead, so we can't ask them. And unfortunately, you're going to have to accept the fact that some of these questions may never be answered."

"I guess. But damn, it sticks in my craw. How could a relative... I mean, I was his nephew."

Dr. Carmichael leaned forward. "You can't trouble yourself with those questions. There will never be an answer to satisfy you. It's highly likely that this man, this Larry, is innocent. There's no way to know if he indeed was one of the perpetrators. But if he was? These men were psychopaths. It wouldn't have mattered if you were his nephew or even his son. He didn't see you as a human being. These men saw you as a toy, a plaything. So don't try to make sense out of it. It's senseless."

"I just want to understand."

"My point is that you can't. The only one who can understand a psychopath is another psychopath. It's better that you don't understand. Trust me. But you do need to accept that. A normal person with a normal personality can never understand the horrors committed by the criminally insane. They're not meant to."

"But why me?"

Dr. Carmichael shook her head. "That's another question that may never be answered. You were in the right place at the right time. Or rather the wrong place at the wrong time."

"If only I hadn't gone looking for Luke."

"But you did. And you suffered the consequences. 'What ifs' don't do anyone any good, Talon. All you can do is accept the past and move forward."

I knew that. God, I'd heard it enough—not just from Dr.

Carmichael, but from my brothers.

"You say I've come a long way. What makes you say that? I don't feel particularly different."

"Are you kidding? You've come a very long way. You can now talk about this without losing consciousness or sending yourself into a flashback. That's huge."

True. The first time I'd come to see Dr. Carmichael, I'd ended up in the ER after a fainting spell. She was right.

"And you've opened up. You've told Jade you love her. You've told your sister about your experiences."

"And I've been able to say I'm sorry."

"Did that trouble you before?"

I nodded. "It's not that I wasn't sorry. And it's not that I didn't know when I should be sorry. It's just that I had to force the words out."

"And it's easier now?"

"Yeah, I don't know why, but it is."

"I think I know why that is."

"Why?"

She looked me straight in the eye. "Because you stopped blaming others. You've stopped resenting others because this didn't happen to them. It happened to you."

I looked down at my hands clenching the armchair. Had I done that? Had I really? I closed my eyes. "That's a heavy statement to make, Doctor."

"Yes, it is. And look at how you're dealing with it. Your fingers are clenched around that armchair, but you're not storming out of here. You're not yelling at me that I'm wrong. That's got to say something."

"I never thought..."

"Of course you didn't. This would've been on an entirely

subliminal level. Look at your brothers, for example. You love them, and you never thought you blamed them for any of this. But deep inside, you resented that it had to happen to you instead of them."

"That's not true. I'm really glad this didn't happen to either of my brothers. I mean that."

"I know you do. That's not what I mean. You wouldn't wish this on anyone. I absolutely believe that. But in the back of your mind, you were resentful. You were resentful that it was you. Why not someone else? Why not some other kid you didn't even know? You may be thankful that it wasn't Ryan or Jonah, but in the back of your mind, you wonder, why not one of them? Why did it have to be you?"

Could she be right? "And you think that explains why I had such a problem saying I was sorry?"

"I think it explains it very well. Don't you?"

I shook my head, my lips trembling. "God, I never meant to..."

"I know. The subconscious mind is very powerful, though. And the good news is that you're healing. Now you can tell people you're sorry. You're moving forward. You *will* heal."

"I hope so. I've been carrying this burden for so long. I never thought I would ever be free of it. I don't know that I ever can be totally free of it."

"No, you'll never be completely free of it. It will always be part of your history, part of your psyche, part of what makes you Talon Steel. But what you *can* do is let it stay in your past, move forward, let yourself love and be loved. You've come such a long way already. I know it may not feel like you have, but just the fact that you can say you're sorry to someone. That's huge."

Was she right? And then something dawned on me—like

a light bulb moment. I was amazed I hadn't realized it before now. "Wow," I said aloud.

"What is it?"

"I can't remember the last time I went to the kitchen at night to stare at a glass of water."

★ ★ ★ ★

The experts I'd retained before I went to Dr. Carmichael's met me at Shem's body shop at seven. We entered around back, and Shem let us in the locked gate.

"The car's over here," Shem said.

He led us to a black Bentley. A fucking Bentley. I was no stranger to nice cars, though I preferred my old pickup to my Mercedes-Benz.

"Shem," I said, "thanks for letting us in. This is Bill Friedman and Clark Tyson. They've agreed to take a look and see if the airbag was tampered with."

"Go right ahead," Shem said.

"Thanks." I handed Shem some bills. "For your trouble."

"I'll just be over here looking the other way." He ambled back inside the shop.

The two guys looked at the car for about half an hour and then came back to me.

"I wish we had better news for you, Mr. Steel," Friedman said. "Because the car has been completely rebuilt since the accident and a new airbag put in, there's just no way to tell if the original was tampered with. Do you think Shem in there has the original airbag? The one that didn't deploy?"

"I don't have a clue, but we can ask him."

I motioned to Shem through the window.

He came out. "Yeah?"

"The guys here can't find any problem with the airbag. Nothing indicated it had been tampered with."

"I was afraid of that. I mean, we completed the work. We had no reason to suspect any wrongdoing, so we didn't look for anything."

"Do you have the original airbag? The one that didn't deploy? I assume you put in a new functioning airbag."

"We sure did. I'll have to look around and see if we still have the old airbag. It was trash. I don't know why we would have kept it."

"Do you remember anything odd about the airbag when you removed it?" Friedman asked.

"Can't say that I do, but again, I wasn't looking for anything."

"Sensor could've been bad, or the airbag could've been an old airbag with holes in it," Tyson said. "Anything like that?"

Shem shook his head again. "I wish I could help you fellows. But like I said, we weren't looking for anything."

"Likely you'd have noticed if the airbag was bad itself," Friedman said. "I'm going to have to assume it might've been a faulty sensor. And now that the new one's been installed, we have no way of proving the sensor was faulty in the first place. Even if it was a faulty sensor, that doesn't mean someone put it there. It's a machine. Parts go bad on their own sometimes."

I sighed. "Do normal people off the street know how to put in airbag sensors?"

Shem laughed. "Are you kidding? We get so many doctors and lawyers in here who don't have a clue. I used to work as a mechanic before I got into bodywork. It's amazing how the most intelligent people in the world know nothing about cars."

"Then it's doubtful that the owner of the car could've fiddled with the sensor himself." I was thinking aloud. I'd have to find out who had serviced this car in the past. I turned to Friedman and Tyson. "Gentlemen, I appreciate your time. Very much." I handed them each an envelope full of cash.

"Thank you, Mr. Steel," Friedman said. "I wish we had better news for you."

"It was a long shot. I appreciate you coming out on a Saturday evening."

I said my goodbyes to all three and got in my car. Somehow, I had to figure out where that car had been serviced in the past. And if Nico Kostas was who I thought he was, and if he had done what I thought he'd done, the trail would be difficult—damned near impossible—to pick up.

CHAPTER TWENTY-THREE

Jade

"Hello, Ted."

"Jade, how is your mother?"

I didn't think for a minute that he gave a damn about my mother. "She's doing well. Out of the woods."

"Good, good. Glad to hear it. I suppose the cops have talked to you by now?"

"I'm sure you know that they have. I'm sure they've given you a full report."

Ted cleared his throat. "Yes, of course."

"So what is it that you want?"

"Information, Jade. You and those Steel punks—"

"Excuse me?"

He cleared his throat again. "The Steel brothers. You and the Steel brothers were the last to see my son."

My nerves jumped. Where could Colin be? "That doesn't mean any of us know anything about where he is."

Silence for a moment. Then, "I understand you are now dating Talon Steel, the one who attacked my son."

Good news traveled fast. I was the one who'd wanted to make the relationship public. I guess I'd asked for this. Ted Morse, with his blue-blooded money, could've hired a PI to find out anyway. "Yes, Talon and I are involved."

"Interesting..."

"I don't see why it would be of any interest to you."

"Just a little bit interesting to me that my son's former fiancée and the man who attacked him, who is now dating said former fiancée, were the last two people to see him alive."

"There's no reason to believe he's not still alive, Ted."

"Still, coincidental, isn't it?"

This man had known me for seven years. The nerve! I knew better than to say anything else. "This conversation is over." I ended the call. Chills raked over my body. I had no idea where Colin was, and though I didn't particularly care where he was, I did want him to be okay. But the nerve of that man, to accuse Talon and me.

The attorney in me advised caution. I would not speak again to Ted Morse. Would not take any of his calls. He wanted to talk to me? He'd have to have the police arrest me and question me. And I wouldn't be saying a word without an attorney present. That O'Keefe guy had done pretty well for Talon. Of course, I'd been the one to bring the deal to him, but he was the best in Snow Creek as far as I knew. I'd give him a call on Monday and tell him about the situation. And just in case, I'd call Sherry Malone in Denver. I'd been her law clerk, and she was the best of the best.

Just what I didn't need.

Where the hell was Colin? None of this made any sense. Then again, I wouldn't put it past him to just disappear for the hell of it. He'd probably flown off to Cancun to spend some of Daddy's money on booze and hookers.

Thank God he had walked out on me on our wedding day. What would my life have been like if I had married him? I shuddered just thinking about it.

"Everything okay, sweetie?" my dad asked.

I nodded. I wasn't going to burden him with this crap, not while he was still worried about my mother. "Just Colin's dad again, still looking for him."

"That is weird that he just disappeared."

"You're telling me." I wished like anything that Talon and I had not been two of the last people to see him. This wasn't going to lead to anything good.

I needed to change the subject. I'd had enough of Colin to last a lifetime. I looked at my watch. "It's seven thirty. Are you hungry?"

My father smiled. "I am. Seems like I couldn't eat at all while it was touch and go with your mother. But now that we know she's going to be okay, I'm famished."

"I'm sure you're sick to death of hospital food by now. Let's go somewhere. I don't know Grand Junction very well, but there's got to be a decent restaurant around here. And I just got paid."

"Aren't you saving up for a down payment on a car?"

"Yes, but now I'm acting city attorney. I got a little raise. I think it's enough to treat my dad to a nice meal."

"Sweetie, I'm happy to pick up the tab."

"Are you kidding? I've been waiting for the day when I can treat you. I'm happy to do it. What are you in the mood for? I'll Google the area and see what I come up with."

"Heck, you know me. I'm happy with a burger and fries."

"Yeah, I am too. I guess my mother's champagne taste didn't pass to me."

"Or your father's beer budget had a lot to do with how your tastes were formed."

I laughed and looked down at my phone. "There's an

Italian place not too far away. Of course I'm sure they're not nearly as good as anything Marj or Felicia can make."

"Felicia?"

"She's the Steels' cook and housekeeper. Man, that woman can cook."

"Italian sounds good, sweetie. Let's go there."

★ ★ ★ ★

I was halfway through my veal piccata when my phone buzzed on the table. I took a sip of my Chianti—which wasn't nearly as good as Ryan's Italian blend—and said to my father, "Mind if I take this?"

"Of course not." He shoveled another forkful of spaghetti and meatballs into his mouth. That was my dad—a full array of Italian haute cuisine, and he chose spaghetti and meatballs. And I loved him for it. I smiled as I picked up my phone—

My heart nearly stopped. Colin's number. "Hello? Colin?"

Silence.

"Colin? Talk to me. Everyone's worried about you. Where are you?"

Still nothing, until the line went dead.

CHAPTER TWENTY-FOUR

Talon

I texted Jade to let her know I was still in the city. Told her I had some business keeping me here. It wasn't a lie. I'd had a therapy session and then met with the guys about Kostas's car. She texted me back that she and her father were at an Italian restaurant near the hospital and invited me to meet them there. So here I was, walking into Milano's.

I found Jade and her dad and sat down between them at their four-top. Her father was looking at her, his eyebrows arched.

"That was Colin," she said.

My nerves prickled. "What?"

"She just got a call," Brian said. "Are you sure it was his number?" he asked her.

"Yeah. Unless he changed it. But then, who else would be calling me from his old number? This is great. It means he's most likely alive." She shook her head. "Thank God. If only he'd talked to me.

"He didn't say anything?" I asked.

"No, he didn't. Is there any way to have this call traced?"

"I don't know," Brian said. "And there's something else you haven't thought of."

"What's that?" Jade clutched the stem of her wineglass.

"It wasn't necessarily Colin calling. All we know is that it was Colin's phone."

Their waitress interrupted us. They were both nearly done with their meals, so I ordered some chicken Marsala and a glass of Chianti.

"You definitely need to call the cops," I said after the waitress left.

"I will," Jade replied, "but all I have is Steve Dugan's card with his office number on it."

"No problem," I said. "Steve's a poker buddy of mine. I have his cell number. I'll call him now."

Jade bit her lip. "It's nine o'clock on a Saturday night, Talon."

"So what? He's been investigating this guy's disappearance, and we just got a lead. Let's let him know." I quickly pulled up Steve's number.

"Hello?"

"Hey, Steve. Talon Steel."

"Hey, Tal, what's going on?"

"Jade just got a call from Colin Morse's phone."

"What?" Steve nearly took my ear off.

"Yeah. We're in Grand Junction, where her mom is in the hospital. About an hour ago, she got a call from Colin's phone, but no one said anything, and then the phone eventually went dead. Any way you can trace where it came from?"

"Hell, yeah. I just need Jade's number and the time of the call. We should be able to find something."

I quickly gave him the information he needed.

"I'll let you know if this leads to anything."

"Okay, thanks. At least we know it was his number. Of course, it could have been anyone using his phone."

"True enough," Steve said. "I'll get on it and let you know if it leads to anything."

"Great. Thanks, Steve."

By the time I was done with my phone call, my chicken Marsala had arrived. Not as good as Felicia's or my sister's, but not bad. Besides, I was starving. I hadn't eaten anything all day.

I thought about whether to tell Jade about what I'd been investigating this evening but decided against it. No need to worry her or her father right now.

I felt a little awkward sitting next to Jade's father, but the two of them talked a lot, so I was content to eat my food and say very little. When I was finally done, I insisted on picking up the check, although Jade fought me on it. Finally I won out.

Jade's dad had driven her over here from the hospital.

"Do you want to get a room for the night?" I asked her. "Or do you want me to drive you back to the ranch?"

"Since my mom is doing okay, I think I want to go back to my apartment tonight. Not the ranch. I don't have anything there."

A lump clogged my throat. "Okay." I turned to her dad and shook his hand. "It was nice meeting you, Brian."

"You too, Talon."

Jade and I didn't talk much on the ride home. She was clearly exhausted, and so was I. I hadn't slept at all last night because I had been on the computer researching those bastards.

I ended up dropping Jade off at her apartment and kissing her goodbye. As much as I wanted to make love to her, I was just too tired, so I gave her a deep kiss and then left to drive home.

★ ★ ★ ★

On Monday morning, I was back at Dr. Carmichael's office.

"I tell you, Doc, I really want to find out something about that third man. The one with the low voice. I think I may have identified the one with the tattoo and the one missing his toe. Of course, both of them have now disappeared. One way or another, I'm going to find all of them."

"You're very determined, which is a good thing. Remember, though, that only a few weeks ago, you weren't sure you wanted to try to catch these guys. Don't your drive for vengeance keep you from your goal, which is healing."

"Don't you think seeing the perpetrators behind bars will be healing for me?"

"It may not hurt your progress, but it won't help your healing as much as you think it will. And if you become distracted and neglect your healing, yes, it could hinder you."

"How can you say that?"

"Let's put it this way. Say you're a mother whose child was murdered. Or a father, for that matter. And the perpetrator is caught and convicted and will now spend the rest of his life in prison. Does that make you feel any better?"

"I would think it would."

"Will it bring the child back?"

"Well, no, of course not."

"Remember why you're here. Seeking justice and putting your abductors behind bars won't change what they did to you, Talon. Yes, I want them behind bars. I want them to pay for what they did to you and to all those other children. And I also want to know that they're behind bars so they can't hurt any other children as well. But that won't change what you went through."

"Jesus, Doc."

"Please don't misunderstand me. I'm not in any way belittling your need to see justice served. I want to see justice served as much as you do. But whether or not those men are caught won't change what happened to you and won't really have any effect on your healing."

"That doesn't seem possible."

"You can't see it now because they're still at large. But believe me. I've had so many patients who think that once they put someone who did them wrong behind bars, they'll feel so much better. They don't. It doesn't work that way. Believe me, I wish it did. Of course, then I'd be out of a job." She smiled.

I thought for a minute. What if someone had killed someone I loved? One of my brothers or my sister? Or—*God*—Jade? Would I feel any better seeing the killer behind bars? It wouldn't bring Jade back.

"Okay, Doc, I see what you're getting at."

"I'm not telling you to stop trying to catch them and bring them to justice. Just don't confuse that with your own healing."

"Gotcha."

"So you want to try to remember something about the third man, the one you referred to as Low Voice?"

I nodded. "The only thing constant about that entire time was the phoenix tattoo. But then recently I remembered that one of the others was missing a toe. So it seems possible that I might be able to remember something about the third one."

"It's certainly possible. But the phoenix tattoo and the missing toe are both very distinct physical characteristics about two people that most people don't have. What if this third person didn't have a distinct characteristic like that?"

"Surely there must be something I could remember about him. I mean, he did have a low voice."

"But you said yourself that you're remembering this as a ten-year-old, and your voice was still prepubescent. So all we really know is that this guy's voice was lower than the other two."

"Don't try to talk me out of this, Doc."

She smiled. "Talon, I would never try to talk you out of anything. But I just want you to understand going in that there may not be anything distinct about the third guy. What are the chances that all three of these men have some distinguishing characteristic?"

"I've got to try. I've just got to."

"All right. Would you like to try guided hypnosis again? I have to warn you, Talon, it won't be like the last time. Last time we went back to a dream you had recently. This time I would have to take you back to when you were ten years old, to witness the horrors that actually took place. Are you ready for that?"

I closed my eyes and breathed in deeply. Slowly I let my breath out, willing my hands to unclench from the armchair. I had to do this. Maybe finding those fuckers wouldn't heal me, but at least I'd know they were getting their just desserts. I opened my eyes and stared at Dr. Carmichael with all the intensity I could muster. "I'm sure. Let's do it, Doc."

★ ★ ★ ★

Sometimes I dreamed about a beach. We didn't go to the beach much, but I'd been a few times in both Florida and California. I'd seen both oceans. Nothing was more fun than the waves. Joe and Ryan and I used to love playing in the waves, getting our trucks filled with sand, yet still going back for more.

My mother would call out, "Ryan, don't go in any farther!"

But my little brother was not to be left behind. He followed me everywhere. And I in turn followed Joe. The beach was fun. The sound of the waves, the smell of the sand, the coconut oil sunscreen, the fish. Sometimes I walked off by myself, looking for shells. Joe and Ryan weren't interested in that, especially Joe. My big brother loved the water and stayed in it the entire time we were at the beach. Although Ryan wasn't as drawn to the water as Joe was, he had no interest in collecting shells, so walking along the beach was the one place Ryan didn't follow me. I liked being alone. My little brother got on my nerves most of the time.

Sometimes I would lie on my beach towel and just let the sun shine on my wet body.

As I was doing now.

I let the rays soak into me, let their warmth infuse me.

Had I ever been this relaxed before? Maybe when I was riding a horse. But not any other time.

Sometimes I wished we didn't live in Colorado. The mountains were beautiful and I loved them, but there was something about the beach...

Until I was plucked from my beach towel.

"You ready for some action, boy?" the one with the low voice said.

"I'm hungry," I squeaked out.

"We fed you, didn't we, boy?"

I couldn't remember the last time I'd eaten. I'd lost track. Sometimes the third one, the one who seemed more like a follower, the one who was missing a toe, brought me three meals *a day. Other times he didn't come at all. And even if he did, I often threw up what I ate.*

"You be a good little pussy for us, and we'll bring you a steak dinner." Low Voice cackled in my ear. "Would you like that, boy? Big juicy steak dinner?"

I closed my eyes.

"Get him ready for me," said another evil voice.

Tattoo. His voice was the slimiest, the most demonic, the most evil. If it had a color, it would be black with red splotches. That's the color I imagined when I heard him speak, as if evil were speaking.

And of course it was evil speaking.

I had ceased thinking of these three people as human. No human could do what they did.

I was biding my time. How long would it be before they got tired of me, killed me, and chopped me into splintering pieces like they had done to Luke?

I hoped it would be soon.

"I'll get him ready for you," Low Voice said. "I'll get him nice and lubed up."

I trembled, my body quaking. I didn't want to tremble, but my body did it of its own accord. It wasn't like I didn't know what was going to happen. Not like the first time, when they had completely surprised me, completely destroyed my belief in anything good in the world.

"Assume the position, bitch," Low Voice said.

Assume the position. Those dreaded words. It meant to get on my hands and knees.

I braced for the pain. The inevitable pain.

But it wasn't the pain I felt first. It was his hot, rank breath on the back of my neck. Raspy breath, wheezing, a timeless breeze as I waited, suspended, for the sharp pain that would soon come. Like a metal spike, it did come. And I cried out.

"That's it, bitch. Yeah," Low Voice groaned.

I detached. Like I always did. Although it wasn't Tattoo, I always went to the bird. Colorful bird that I could focus on to get through the pain, the humiliation.

I had learned to see the bird on all of their forearms. And it helped.

So I focused on it, willing my mind to soar out of my body, like the phoenix rising from its ashes. Was the only way to get through it.

Though outside my body, I heard myself cry out.

They liked it when I cried out. If I didn't, they would clock me upside the head or beat my ass. More pain, more humiliation. Still, I'd have given anything not to cry out, not to give them that satisfaction.

I was the little bitch they said I was. I couldn't control my reactions.

God... God...

"No, no, no, no, no!"

★ ★ ★ ★

I was back in Dr. Carmichael's office, clenching the chair, perspiration emerging on my forehead and dripping down my cheeks.

Or was it tears?

"Easy, Talon," she said in a soothing voice. "We don't have to go back if you don't want to."

"God. I was there. I was fucking there."

"You were. We were making progress."

"What pulled me out?"

"You pulled yourself out. Normally I would bring you out slowly. But remember what I said the first time we tried this? That you would be able to come out anytime if you needed to? That's what happened. So now you know that you can."

I breathed in and out rapidly, panting like a damned dog. I had been there like it was fucking yesterday. That motherfucker, the low-voiced one who I had no memories of. He was right there, over me, and I was focusing on his forearm, his blank forearm.

Nothing. Nothing stood out. At least not yet.

I had to go back.

I didn't want to, but I had to.

"Take me back, Doc."

"Are you sure?"

I nodded. "I have to. There has to be something."

★ ★ ★ ★

No beach this time. I was back in that dank cellar, Low Voice over me.

Still detached, seeing the bird on his blank forearm...

Look around, an inner voice said to me. Look around and see what's here.

His left forearm was blank. He was wearing all black. Black short sleeves, like always. Always black with black masks. The only one who sometimes wore something different was the third one, the follower, the lemming.

I'd never seen the other two in anything but black. Sometimes T-shirts, sometimes wife-beaters. T-shirt today.

Though it pained me to do so, I forced my gaze from the

invisible fiery bird on his left forearm. I couldn't see much. He was on top of me, so my visual field was limited. His hands. Fingernails oddly clean and well kept. Long thin fingers, but nothing unusual. I looked over to his other hand, his other arm on the right side.

"Yeah, bitch, I'm getting ready. I'm getting fucking ready."

"Lube him up good for me," Tattoo said again.

Bile rose in my throat, but I swallowed it down. I didn't want to get beaten for throwing up.

I'd throw up anyway. I always did. But I was usually able to wait until they left.

His right hand looked the same. Long fingers, clean fingernails. Forearm was also blank. I let my gaze wander up to his upper arm.

And now he wasn't wearing a T-shirt anymore. He was wearing a black wife-beater. How had that changed?

I was going crazy. Bat-shit crazy. My mind didn't know what was real and what was unreal anymore. Walls closed in on me at night, the bird emerged and taunted me. It all seemed very real.

So it made perfect sense to me that the T-shirt had turned into a wife-beater. His upper arm was right at my eye level.

And then I saw it.

A patch of darker skin. A birthmark, on the inside of his arm, very close to his armpit.

It was shaped like something I'd seen before.

An odd shape. Where had I seen it?

"Ah!" He groaned, thrusting.

And then relief.

It still hurt, and I knew it would only be mere seconds before someone else was abusing me, but for these few sacred seconds when he slid out of me, I actually felt relief.

He was gone.

The shape... Where had I seen it before?

Where had I seen it before?

And then the pain was gone. As if it had never been there. I was back lying on my soft beach towel under the California sun. In the distance, my brothers laughed, splashing each other. I opened my eyes and looked next to me. My beautiful mother sat there, reading a book. Her long brown hair was pulled back in a ponytail out of her face, and she wore a wide-brimmed hat and sunglasses.

She was beautiful, my mother. So beautiful.

I turned the other way, and my big strong father was on my other side. He wasn't reading. He was watching my brothers. My father never took his eyes off us. If we did something wrong, no matter how sneaky we were, he knew.

He watched us constantly.

It was annoying, but I also knew how much he loved us.

We were loved.

I was loved.

I closed my eyes again and let the warmth of the sun envelop me.

★ ★ ★ ★

When I opened my eyes, I was back in Dr. Carmichael's office, back in the recliner. Oddly, I wasn't clenching the arms.

I looked over at her. "I remember something."

CHAPTER TWENTY-FIVE

Jade

After I had finished my morning court appearances, I decided to do a little investigation of my own—not on the Steels as I'd been instructed to do by Larry. After all, Larry was no longer here. He had disappeared, just like Nico Kostas and Colin had.

It didn't seem possible that Larry and Nico could've had anything to do with Colin's disappearance. I hadn't heard anything yet from Steve Dugan over at the station about whether my phone call had led to anything. If he didn't call me by the end of the day, I was going to give him a call.

In the meantime, I had some time available, so I decided to do some investigation of Nico Kostas. But no sooner had I started, than I stopped. I had been so upset about Larry bending the rules and bending his ethics when he was city attorney. Now here I was, acting city attorney, and I was investigating something that had nothing to do with my job at the moment.

Damned if I was going to be that kind of an attorney. If I had to, I would do my research here at the office, but I would do it on my own time, after hours. No one would think anything of it if I stayed late working on cases. For now, I was the acting city attorney, and I would behave as such.

A couple hours later, when I'd finished everything on my own agenda for the day, I went back to the last assignment

Larry had given me. To investigate the Steels.

He had started out by giving me folders and folders full of bank accounts. The only thing out of the ordinary that I'd found was a five-million-dollar transfer about twenty-five years ago.

One thing I had learned about the Steels—they weren't above paying to get what they wanted.

That five million dollars had gone somewhere, and I was going to find out where.

Talon had told me once that something horrible had happened to him. I couldn't begin to imagine what it might've been, but I wondered if it had been twenty-five years prior. What could've happened that the Steels would've been willing to pay five million dollars to cover up?

I didn't have any idea, but I could start by trying to find out where that five million had gone.

As much as I knew she never wanted to hear from me again, I decided to call Wendy Madigan, the former National News correspondent who had helped shed some light on the Steels a few weeks earlier. I found her number and picked up the phone.

"Ms. Roberts."

I couldn't help smiling. "Thank you for picking up the phone, Wendy. Since you obviously knew it was me, I'm surprised you did."

A sigh met my ears. "I really do wish I could help you. Rather, I wish I could go back in time and do things differently."

"Would that include your affair with Bradford Steel?"

Another sigh. "No. As much as I hated the idea of being the other woman, Brad and I... Well, we had a connection that I think few people ever find. It was like we knew each other in a previous life or something. Our souls were connected." And one more sigh. "I don't mean to sound all esoteric. I'm actually a pretty level-headed and down-to-earth person." She let out a chuckle.

"I know you are. I know from our previous talks and also from the fact that you were a newswoman. You had to be pretty grounded to do that."

"I'm glad you can see that side of me. I honestly do wish I could help you. I wish I could help those boys and their sister. There was no love lost between me and their mother, but I adored their father. He was everything to me. Those boys... God, they all look just like him."

"So I've heard. Marjorie tells me she's the only one who bears even a slight resemblance to their mother. And that's just in the shape of her face and lips. Otherwise she's a female version of her brothers."

"If you had known Brad, it would make perfect sense to you why his genes were so dominant. That's the kind of man he was. Dominant. Controlling, but in a completely loving way." She sighed once more. "Why am I even telling you all this?"

I wasn't sure why she was either, but I wanted her to continue. Desperately. "If it helps to talk about it, please do. I'll be happy to keep your confidence. I'm really only interested in helping the Steels."

"Well, to be honest with you, I get a good feeling from you, Jade. I know you're Marjorie's best friend, and you wouldn't hurt her. I have no idea why your boss wants to investigate the Steels."

Something in her tone made me pause—as if maybe she *did* know why my boss wanted to investigate the Steels.

"Can you tell me a little more about Bradford Steel?

Marjorie doesn't talk a lot about him, and of course she doesn't remember her mother all."

"All I can tell you is that he was like no one I'd ever known before. His presence, his mere stance, denoted strength, everything a man should be. I can't explain it any better than that, and I'm sure you don't understand what I mean."

Oh, but I did understand. Clearly Talon was quite a bit like his father. And from what I could tell, both of his brothers were too, in more than just looks.

"Have you ever been in love, Jade? Have you ever been willing to do anything for another person? Have you ever been willing to give your whole life to someone else? Because that's how it was with Brad and me. And I feel confident in saying that he felt the same way I did. If Daphne hadn't gotten pregnant with the oldest son, I don't think they would've married."

Oh, how well I did know. And maybe it was time to open up to Wendy, especially since she was opening up to me. Besides, Talon had said we could take our relationship public.

"Wendy, I actually know exactly how you feel. I really do. And the reason I know that..." I cleared my throat and drew in a deep breath. This was the right thing to do. "I've kept your confidence. I ask that you keep mine."

"Of course," she said.

"The reason I understand is, I'm in love. With Talon Steel."

Silence on the other end of the line.

"I suppose that's a lot to take in," I said.

"No, it's not that. It's just..."

"Just what?"

"Talon has...issues."

That was the understatement of the world. "I know. He's

in therapy."

"Has he told you? I mean, *why* he's in therapy?"

It occurred to me that I could say yes. Then Wendy would spill some information that she thought I had. But I couldn't do that to Talon. I had promised that I wouldn't pressure him, that I would let him tell me whatever he needed to tell me in his own time. So I turned off the attorney in me. "No, he hasn't. He's just not ready yet, and I've promised him that I won't pressure him."

"I would tell you if I could."

"Yes, I believe you would. But don't. I owe Talon more than that. I owe him my trust. If he's ever going to trust me the way I trust him, he needs to know that I'm not trying to find out what's going on behind his back."

"It sounds like he's lucky to have you, Jade."

"I don't know about that. I can only tell you that what I have with Talon sounds a lot like what you had with his father. He fills a room with his presence, with his strength and dominance."

Wendy let out a laugh. "And it can get pretty fun in the bedroom, can't it?"

My cheeks warmed. I hadn't expected her to get that personal. "Well, without divulging anything private, I can agree with that."

"Like father like son."

I could almost see her smiling through the phone.

As fun as this conversation had the capacity to be, it was getting far beyond why I had called Wendy in the first place. "I believe Talon will tell me when he's ready. And in the meantime, I'm not going to try to flush out anything he's not ready to tell me about. But I am concerned. My boss, for whatever reason, wants information on the Steels. And let me be honest with you. I don't know exactly why. All he told me was that it was classified. He said it was possible that they might be involved with organized crime and money laundering."

Wendy gasped. "That's ridiculous."

"Honestly, Wendy, I don't think they have anything to do with organized crime. I haven't seen anything to indicate that they're involved in anything illegal."

"I can tell you right now that they're not. Neither Brad nor his father would have dealt in any kind of crime or dirty money. They were both true gentlemen. Integrity meant the world to them."

"I believe you." And I did. "But Larry wanted to investigate them for some reason. Do you know what it might be?"

Once again I was met with silence.

"Wendy? You still there?"

"I am," she said softly.

"Well, do you have any ideas?"

"I have some ideas, but I can't tell you without revealing some secrets that I swore never to reveal."

Were they secrets about Talon? Because if they weren't, I didn't understand why she couldn't reveal them. But she had been more than forthcoming with me already. I would not push her.

"Can you at least point me in the right direction?"

"Talon will come to you when he's ready. When he does, and when you've heard his story, call me again."

CHAPTER TWENTY-SIX

Talon

"Relax for a moment. Clear your mind. You just went through a lot. Do some deep breathing, Talon."

I took Dr. Carmichael's advice, breathing in, out. In, out. In, out.

"Now," she said. "Tell me. What do you remember?"

"The one with the low voice. He has a birthmark. Not the red kind, but the kind where your skin is just a little darker."

She nodded. "And where did you see it?"

"On his upper arm. It was the weirdest thing. When I started the flashback, he was wearing a black T-shirt. I couldn't see anything. But then all of a sudden he was no longer wearing a black T-shirt. He was wearing a black tank top. You know, a wife-beater. How could that have happened?"

"I was guiding you. You told me what he was wearing, and I asked if they ever wore anything else. You told me yes, sometimes he wore a black wife-beater. So we manipulated the vision."

"Amazing."

"Hypnosis is a pretty powerful tool, especially when the person really wants to be helped. It's a good sign, Talon."

"The birthmark had a shape. I can't really describe it. Some jagged edges. But it looked like something familiar."

"Would you recognize it if you saw it again?"

"I think so." I looked around her office, thinking, until my gaze settled on the globe atop her desk. I shot upright. I grabbed the globe and brought it over to her, pointing to North America. "Texas. It looked like the state of Texas."

"Exactly like the state of Texas?"

"Of course not. But it reminded me of that. All I could think of when I was in the flashback was that I had seen the shape before or something like it before." I pointed again. "And this is it."

"All right. Where was this birthmark?"

"His upper arm, on the inside, almost to his armpit." I put the globe on the coffee table in front of us. "Why didn't I ever remember that?"

"Talon, you blocked a lot of this out. It was only recently that you remembered one of them was missing a toe. That's completely normal."

"But if I blocked that out, why couldn't I block out the worst? Why do I remember every single time they came to me, every single time they hurt me? Wouldn't it have made more sense to block that out?"

"The mind is a unique thing, Talon. I can't tell you why you remembered some things and not others. What I can tell you is that during the time you were in captivity, you were hurt. You were hurt a lot by three deranged masked men. You were a ten-year-old boy. All you thought about was that you were hurting. There was no reason for you to notice anything else."

Perhaps she made sense. I didn't know at this point. And besides, how was I going to find a guy with a birthmark that looked like Texas? Of course, I had found a guy with a phoenix tattoo and a guy missing a toe. And even though chances were good that they weren't the right guys, I had a strong feeling they were.

Especially now that both of them had disappeared.

"How will I find that third one?"

"I wish I could tell you. I wish I could guarantee you that every criminal who ever did something heinous to a child would be brought to justice. But unfortunately, we don't live in a perfect world. Many of them go free, and many of them are never caught."

I knew the truth of her words all too well. "I can at least look for the other two."

"Yes, if that will give you peace, by all means, try to find them. But don't let that control your healing. Your healing has nothing to do with them being caught. Remember that."

We had been through that before. "I'd like to believe that, Doc, but if I could beat those two into the next century, I think it would feel pretty damned good."

"And then you'd spend the rest of your life in prison. Is that what you want?"

I shook my head. My whole life up until now had been a prison. And to be locked up? After what I'd been through? Oh, hell, no. "No. I want to live. I want a life. I want a life with Jade."

"Then I think it's time we discussed one other thing."

"What's that?"

"Have you thought about telling Jade? About what happened to you?"

I raked my fingers through my hair. Hell, yes, I'd thought of telling Jade. But it had been hard enough to tell Marjorie. And to see how it affected her. "I don't know. My brothers and I just told our sister, and it didn't go so well."

"What you mean by that?"

"The way she reacted."

"You mean she wasn't supportive?"

"No, nothing like that. She just feels terrible about it. That's the point. She's been sad for days. Tiptoeing around me, like she doesn't know what to say to me or how to act. Which is exactly what I was afraid of."

"That's a normal reaction. She'll be fine. Just give her time."

"But I can't have Jade acting like that around me. Have her feeling sorry for me... God, Doc, I wouldn't be able to take it."

"Who's to say she'll react the same way?"

"You just said it's a very normal reaction."

"It is. But Jade isn't your little sister. She didn't grow up looking up to you, having you as a protector. For Marjorie, her strong older brother has suddenly become—"

"Just stop right there. Don't say 'an object of pity.'"

"No, of course not. What I was going to say is that you've become someone even stronger to her now. And she can't bear the thought of you ever being in pain."

"Why would Jade react any differently?"

"Oh, she'll have the same kind of issues. She won't want to think of you being in any kind of pain, because she loves you. But you're an equal to her. You're not her big brother. It's a different relationship."

"I just don't want her to pity me."

"Then tell her that. She loves you. She doesn't want to hurt you, and if her pity would hurt you, she won't do it."

"Doc. Do you...pity me?"

"That's a loaded question." She sighed. "I feel very bad that you had to go through what you did. But this is my line of work, Talon. You're not the first patient I've seen who suffered a trauma during childhood. And if it helps you, you're not the worst case I've seen, either."

Oddly, that didn't help. Knowing innocent children had lived through worse than I had made me ill. "The person or persons who had a worse time than I did, did they heal? Did they come out of it?"

"Two of them did. And they're leading very successful lives now. But there was one other."

I didn't like where this was going, but I had opened the door. "What happened?"

Dr. Carmichael's eyes glistened. "She wasn't strong enough. She took her own life."

"God. I'm sorry, Doc."

"It's an eye-opening day for a therapist, when you realize that there are some people you just can't help, no matter how hard you try. If I were perfect at my job, perhaps I could've helped her. Or perhaps no therapist on earth could have helped her. I'll never know."

"I'm so sorry."

She sniffed. "It's part of what I do. Not everything can be a success. Doctors lose patients. Businessmen don't always get the deals they want. Lawyers lose cases. It's no different for me. Therapists can't help everyone."

"Still..."

"It's okay, Talon. I've made my peace with it. Or at least as well as I can. I have more successes than I do failures."

"What do you think my outcome will be?"

"I think you're going to be fine. I really do. You've come so far already."

I rubbed my temple. "So now we've come full circle. It's

time to tell Jade."

"Yes, I think it is."

"What if she can't deal with it? What if she leaves me?"

"I don't think she will. But if you want to play the 'what if' game, what if she does? All that tells you is that she wasn't the person you thought she was. And you're better off knowing before you get in any deeper."

"She's told me that whatever it is it won't matter to her. That nothing will ever make her stop loving me."

"Then trust in that. Because if you want a relationship with her, you're going to have to bare your soul."

CHAPTER TWENTY-SEVEN

Jade

Talon invited me over Friday night for dinner. Although I had planned to drive up to the city to see my mom, my dad assured me that everything was fine and told me to have a good time with Talon. Plus, Marj would be in the city for cooking class, and she had promised to stop by to see my mother and give me a detailed report.

So I had relented. I hadn't spent any solid alone time with Talon this week, and I was craving some.

As I was pulling into the ranch, I hoped I had made the right decision. I was determined not to pressure him for information, but if he would just talk to me, I could go back to Wendy Madigan and find out what was truly going on.

Talon and Roger greeted me at the door. I gave Talon a kiss on the lips and Roger a scratch behind the ears.

"It smells great." I inhaled thyme and garlic. "Kind of like a French bistro."

"Felicia made us chateaubriand for two, with green beans and potato gratin."

"Sounds great."

He smiled. "And don't tell Ryan, but we're having real French wine. Château Lascombes, from a very good year."

I let out a small giggle. "My lips are sealed."

He raised an eyebrow. "I hope not. I plan to make good use of those lips later."

My skin tightened around me, and my core throbbed. It had been so long since we'd spent more than just a few minutes together.

"Come on." He led me into the kitchen. "I'll pour you a glass of wine."

I followed. "Are we eating in your room again?"

He shook his head. "No, that didn't go so well the last time, and I didn't want to jinx tonight. We're going to eat out on the deck."

The evening was beautiful. A soft breeze was blowing as we stepped out onto the deck. Talon—or Felicia, probably—had set a lovely little table for two, complete with cloth napkins and sterling silverware. Fine bone china graced the place settings.

"Wow, beautiful," I said.

"This is my mother's wedding china. It's supposed to be worth a fortune, but I don't know. We hardly ever use it, but I wanted tonight to be special."

"Every night we've spent together is special." I lifted my glass and took a sip.

"How's the wine?"

I let the liquid flow over my tongue and down my throat, so soft. "Don't tell Ryan, but it's amazing."

"That's probably because this bottle is nearly as old as Ryan himself." Talon laughed.

"A vintage Bordeaux. I'm not sure I've ever had anything like this."

"Stick with me, blue eyes, and you'll have the best of everything." He pulled me toward him and held me.

He didn't try to kiss me. We just stood in each other's arms for a few timeless moments.

His warmth surrounded me. This was where I was meant to be. With this man. Beside him. His partner going through life. I knew that in the depths of my soul, and though I knew Talon loved me, I still wasn't sure whether he felt exactly the same way. He had so much to work through before we could truly be together.

But tonight was tonight. I wasn't going to spoil it by worrying about where our relationship might be going or what it might not become. Tonight I wanted to enjoy a beautiful dinner with the man I loved. And then I wanted him to take me to his room and fuck me senseless.

Talon urged me to sit down, and then he took my plate and his back into the kitchen. A few moments later, he came back out with two steaming plates full of glorious French food. He bade me to wait another minute, and he came out with two plates of salad and a gorgeous baguette with some European butter.

Talon poured himself a glass of wine, rather than the bourbon I knew he usually preferred. He held up his glass. "To us, blue eyes."

I followed suit and clinked his glass. "To us."

I took another sip of the soft and luxurious wine. Yes, I could get used to living like this.

"Dig in, baby. There's plenty."

After a day of court appearances and no time to stop for lunch, I was famished. I cut a piece of the chateaubriand and dipped it in the sauce.

Oh my God, so good.

"I hope you know that's Steel beef," Talon said, winking.

"Of course. It's the best, right?" I took another bite. So

tender. So flavorful.

"This is the grass-fed beef too, blue eyes."

"I didn't know you raised grass-fed beef."

"It's a specialty line of ours. Joe knows more about it. For an operation as big as ours, it's impossible to raise solely grass-fed beef, but it is better for you, and I think better-tasting. Although all of our beef is awesome."

"It's been awesome every time I've tasted it."

"Tonight, I wanted the best. Grass fed and perfect for my baby."

"So tell me," I said. "When will those amazing Western slope apples and peaches be ready?"

"I am so glad you asked that, blue eyes. Everything's looking good. And Felicia made you a surprise for dessert."

"Oh my God. What?"

He smiled. "You just have to wait and see."

The surprise turned out to be peach pie with Talon's perfect Western slope peaches. I had never tasted anything better. He served me a light dessert wine with it that perfectly complemented the sweet peaches.

"How did I ever think I had tasted peaches before this?" I said, savoring my last bite of pie.

"There's only one thing I can think of that tastes better than my peaches, blue eyes."

"Yeah? What's that?"

"You."

My body heated. The way he was looking at me, I was sure my clothes were melting off from the heat in his gaze. His dark eyes, so full of promise, so full of passion. No one had ever looked at me the way Talon did.

He stood. "Come with me, blue eyes."

"But you haven't finished your pie."

"I've got a taste for something better than pie." He came to me, pulled me out of my chair, and picked me up in his strong arms. Then he walked down the stairs of the deck.

"Aren't we going to your room?" I asked.

"I thought we'd start out here. Such a beautiful night." When we walked below the deck, I spied something the railing had been hiding. An air mattress covered with a soft comforter had been spread out on the lawn. He had made a bed for us. It was the sweetest and sexiest thing I'd ever seen. I let out a sigh, my body melting.

"Talon, that's just lovely."

"Nothing's too good for you, blue eyes.

Another bottle of wine and two glasses sat next to the little bed, along with a picnic basket. I couldn't begin to guess what was inside of it. I was completely sated from dinner, couldn't eat another bite. Unless it was a bite of Talon's succulent flesh.

He took my hand and led me over. "I want to undress you, blue eyes. I want to peel every layer of clothing off of you until you're naked, standing before me, offering yourself to me.

"But we're out in the open, in plain view."

"This is my ranch. No one can see us."

"What about Ryan? In the guest house?"

"First of all, he's half a mile away. And second, I've told him that if he dares come anywhere near this house tonight, I will kick his ass."

I couldn't help but smile.

He cupped my cheek, caressing it with his thumb. "You're so beautiful, Jade. I'm going to undress you slowly. I'm going to savor every inch of you as you bare yourself to me."

I sighed into his palm.

I had come straight from work, and I was wearing a form-fitting stretch dress. But he was not to be deterred. He slid the sleeves over my shoulders and down my arms, slithering the dress over my ample breasts, down my belly, and over my hips. Soon it was a puddle of forest green at my feet. I stood before him now, only in a pink bra and panties and my brown wedge sandals. I silently wished I had worn some black patent-leather stilettos. They would be so much sexier. Of course, I wouldn't have been able to walk all day.

He raked his gaze over me, his eyes blazing with fire. "So beautiful," he said again.

He unclasped my bra and removed it from me, tossing it onto the grass. My breasts fell against my chest, my nipples already hard for him.

Talon licked his lips.

And my body heated.

He skimmed my pink panties over my hips and down around my ankles. I stepped out of them.

"Lie down, blue eyes."

I complied, and he unbuckled my sandals and removed them. My toes were painted a neutral reddish-brown.

"I've never told you how beautiful your feet are, baby."

My feet were just feet. Certainly not my best feature, but not my worst, either. But here was this gorgeous man, worshiping them with his hands. He massaged them gently and then more firmly. I let out a sigh. It felt so good. He kissed each toe as he continued his massage. Then he began moving his hands up my calves, massaging my tired muscles and my thighs.

"Turn over, baby."

I obeyed, and he continued his massage up my calves, up

my thighs, kneading my hamstring and then up to my glutes.

Did he realize what he was doing? He had been in this position, getting a massage from me, when he'd flown off the handle that first time. When I'd...

When I had massaged his anus.

Oh, God.

He said something horrible had happened to him.

Had Talon been...raped? Twenty-five years ago? Dear God, he would've been only ten years old.

My eyes began to flood with tears, but still he was massaging me, groaning endearments to me, telling me how beautiful my body was.

I had to give him this. I had to let him make love to me as he wanted to, here, outside. I couldn't let my fears of what might have happened to him in the past color this night.

He would tell me when he was ready.

He continued massaging up my back, and when he got to my shoulders, I couldn't help but groan. Sitting at a desk all week, whether in my office or at the courthouse, took its toll on my shoulders. I needed to get out and exercise more.

As much as my body heated and throbbed, having him near me, this was more about comfort and love than it was about passion and desire. He was taking care of me, soothing me. And God, I loved him for it.

I was facedown, so he couldn't do anything to my nipples, and he had avoided my pussy on the way up my body. Did he intend to make love to me tonight? It had sounded like that was his intention. He said he wanted to taste something better than the peach pie.

When he was done massaging my shoulders, he worked my neck and then brought his face down so his thick, wavy hair caressed my neck and my cheek.

"I don't think I can explain to you how much you mean to me, blue eyes," he said softly into my hair. "Sometimes I wake up, and I can't believe there's someone like you in the world. It gives me hope, you know?"

I had no idea how to respond to that. I was an ordinary girl—an ordinary girl that was a dime a dozen. There was nothing special about me.

As if reading my mind, he continued, "You *are* special, blue eyes. You've changed me. You've made me see things differently. You've made me want to be a better man. You've made me want to live."

Live? Had he not wanted to live? Iraq... He had wanted to get killed in Iraq...

All these thoughts were jumbled in my head, a mass of cogitation that I couldn't make sense of, especially not while he had calmed my body into a state of blissful relaxation.

"I'm going to be the man you deserve, Jade. I promise you." He brushed his lips softly against my neck. "I promise you that."

I turned over then and met his gaze. "I've never asked you to be anything other than who you are, Talon. You are everything to me." And I spoke the truth.

"I want to make love to you, baby. I want to make love to you out here, in the beautiful outdoors. I want us to make love under the sunset, against the Rocky Mountains. And then, when the sky darkens, and we can see the stars, I need to talk to you."

"I—" I clamped my lips shut.

"What?"

I shook my head. "Nothing." I had been about to say he

could talk to me now. But this had to go at his pace. He needed to be comfortable. Perhaps he needed to be with me, perhaps he needed to release, perhaps he just needed to feel the love the two of us shared. Whatever it was that he needed, I wasn't going to stand in his way. I looked into his blazing brown eyes. "Please. Please, Talon. Make love to me."

CHAPTER TWENTY-EIGHT

Talon

She was so beautiful, lying there, her steely blue eyes so trusting. I would turn her world upside down later, but first, I wanted to make slow, sweet love to her, love like we normally didn't make but love that had its own merits. I liked to dominate her in the bedroom, and she liked submitting to my desires. But this wasn't going to be about that. This would be the two of us as equals, joining our bodies, surrendering to the love between us.

She watched me with those silver-blue eyes as I undressed slowly. She sucked in a breath when I tossed my shirt on the soft grass. I smiled. I loved that she was attracted to me, that my body pleased her.

"You're so gorgeous, Talon," she said.

Her words no longer embarrassed me. They only gave me pleasure, to know that I was making her happy. I took off my boots and socks and then unbuckled my jeans and slid them and my boxers over my hips. When I was naked, I sat down on the bed. She lay on her back, her legs spread slightly, her pink lips glistening, the musk of her sex wafting toward me. I inhaled. God, better than peach pie.

She was wet. I could tell by looking at her hard little nipples, the glassy look in her light-blue eyes. She was wet, and she was ready for me.

So I climbed atop her and slowly slid into her.

That soft sigh escaped her throat, and I closed my eyes, savoring it.

We hadn't kissed. I hadn't sucked or pinched her nipples. She hadn't sucked and licked my cock. All I had done was massage her body, yet we were both ready.

For a moment, I held myself, seated to the hilt inside her warmth, the place where I felt most at home, most right. She completed me. I'd always known I was incomplete because of my past. Never thought I'd be whole. But Jade made me whole. Made me want to be whole.

I pulled out slowly and plunged back in. She sighed beneath me.

"Good, baby?"

"God, yes," she sighed. "So good. You feel so good inside me."

I pulled in and out again slowly, our bodies joining, our love—not our passion and desire—the driving force between us. I used soft strokes, and we looked into each other's eyes, her gaze never wavering. When she curled her lips into a smile, I closed my eyes for just a minute, the most profound sense of love filling every pore in my body.

I reveled in the deep feeling of finally being whole, unbroken. And then I opened my eyes and thrust once more, coming home.

She climaxed around me as I released, both of us panting, moaning, loving each other.

When my climax finally subsided, I rolled off her onto my back. She curled up beside me, snuggling into my arms.

"I love you so much, Talon," she said.

My eyes were closed, my body sated. "I love you too, blue eyes."

We lay there for a while as the sun went down. The sky turned pink and orange and fuchsia, and then silver gray, and the first star sparkled in the night sky.

It was so easy to be with Jade. To just be. We didn't have to be talking, we didn't have to be making love, we didn't have to be doing anything. We could just be together—a state of pure being. Everything felt so right.

But it was time.

If I was going to go the distance with Jade, I had to tell her all my secrets. As much as I didn't want to lay this on her, I had to. And I had to trust that she wouldn't turn away from me.

"Do you want to sit in the hot tub a while?" I asked her.

She let out a yawn. "Sounds heavenly, but it might put me to sleep."

"Good point," I said. "We'll stay here. Do you want something to drink?"

"Maybe another glass of wine. Or some ice water's fine too."

"You got it." I'd get her both. I got up and ambled into the kitchen, naked as a jaybird, for two glasses of ice water. When I returned I poured two glasses of wine and took a plate of strawberries out of the basket by the bed.

"You're a gem," she said, taking first a long sip of water and then a small sip of wine.

"You want a strawberry?" I held one up to her mouth.

She took a delicate bite and licked her lips. "Mmm."

"Jade?"

"Yeah?"

My nerves tensed up. *You don't have to do this, Talon. You can put it off.* No. I had to. I had come so far. I cleared my throat.

"Remember when I told you something happened to me when I was younger? Something horrible?"

She set her glass down on the tray and snuggled up to me, laying her head on my shoulder. "I will listen to whatever you have to say, Talon. I want you to tell me if you're ready. But I need you to trust in one thing."

"What's that?"

"Nothing will ever change the way I feel about you. Nothing will ever change how much I love you."

And in that moment, trapped in her steely blue gaze, I believed her.

I trusted her.

"It happened twenty-five years ago. I was ten."

★ ★ ★ ★

She stayed quiet beside me, letting me talk. She didn't interrupt. She didn't ask questions. She let me say my piece. And although she sniffed and I felt her tears trickle against my shoulder, still she stayed quiet, and still I continued.

The words came out of me robotically, without emotion. In truth, I forced it that way. If I had let emotion into it, I wouldn't have gotten through it. When I was finally finished, she pulled away from me and sat up.

And I saw what I feared most.

The look of pity in her silver-blue eyes.

My ire rose. "Jade, I didn't tell you this so you could pity me."

"Is that what you think?" She bit her lip.

"I recognize that look. Yours is not the first face I've seen it on. I see it on the face of any person who knows the truth about me."

"Talon, sit up. Sit up and look at me."

I did as she asked. I sat up on the air mattress and faced her.

She shook her head. "No, damn it. I mean look at me. *Really* look at me."

I didn't know what she was asking. "I am looking at you. You're beautiful. But I hate the fact that I caused you tears."

She grabbed me by the shoulders, something she'd never done before. Then she cupped my cheeks and brought her forehead to mine. "Damn it, Talon. What you see in my eyes is not pity. These tears are not tears of pity. These tears are for a ten-year-old little boy who went through hell and came out of it. These are tears of sadness for what that little boy went through and tears of joy for the man he became—the man I love more than anything."

"I was so afraid to tell you."

"Why?"

"I thought you might—" I swallowed the lump clogging my throat. "I thought you might turn away from me."

She pulled back a ways. "How could you think that? How could you think so little of me? Don't you believe in the love I have for you?"

I let out a sigh. "Maybe at first I didn't. But I do now, Jade. I believe in your love for me. And I believe in my love for you. You're the reason I..."

"What?"

I drew in a breath and let it out slowly, bracing myself, preparing for the words I needed to say to her. "You, Jade. You know how I tried to get my ass blown off while I was over in

Iraq?"

"Yes."

"When I met you, when I realized there was someone in the world like you, I was really glad I hadn't been killed. I wanted to live. For you. For Joe and Ryan and Marj. And most of all, blue eyes, for me. You helped me see that my life still had worth, that it was worth trying to work through all the crap that I've gone through. Because you deserve the best. You deserve a man who is not broken. And blue eyes, if it takes me the rest of my life, I am going to heal. I'm going to heal so I can be the man you deserve."

CHAPTER TWENTY-NINE

Jade

My heart was breaking. Talon didn't need my pity. He'd said as much. Now, everything he'd ever said, everything he'd ever done since we first met made so much sense. My beautiful man. I ached for the little boy he was, to have his innocence stolen in such a horrific and violating way.

But he was here. And he was mine. And goddamnit, I would see that he got through this.

"What are you thinking, blue eyes?"

"I'll be honest. I have a lot of questions. Not just about what you've been through but about your life, your therapy. But I don't want to push you. I want you to tell me things when you're ready to tell me."

"I've told you everything. Everything that I remember. I seem to come up with new stuff in therapy all the time. But I am surprised you haven't asked about a few things."

"What's that?" I asked.

"The phoenix tattoo. And the missing little toe."

I gasped. I had been so shaken up by Talon's story that I hadn't put two and two together yet. No wonder he was so interested in Nico Kostas and Larry Wade. He thought they were two of his attackers.

"Oh my God, Talon. I'm so sorry."

"What do you mean?"

"I almost got that tattoo." I burst into tears. "Oh my God, what if Marjorie hadn't called that night? What if I had that thing permanently fixed on my body? Oh, God. Oh my God."

Tears fell from my eyes, liquid poured from my nose, and soon I was congested. I was racking with sobs. I threw myself down onto the comforter on the air bed, weeping into it.

What would that have done to Talon? What would it have done?

Strong hands did not caress my body. Talon did not offer me comfort. I didn't expect him to. This was self-indulgence, pure and simple. I needed to get hold of myself. This was not about me. This was about Talon. This was not about the tattoo I hadn't gotten, thank God. How selfish was I?

I gulped down my last sob and sat back up. "I'm so sorry, Talon. I don't know what came over me."

"It's okay, blue eyes. It's okay to cry for me. For a long time I thought it wasn't okay. I thought it made me weak. But I've shed my share of tears since then—during therapy and just dealing with it on my own."

"You said you didn't want my pity."

"I don't. But if those tears come from your love for me, how can I hate them? I love you, and I'm sorry you have to hurt because of what happened to me."

"Oh, Talon, you have nothing to be sorry for. I'm the one who's sorry. Thank God I didn't get that tattoo."

"I've been thinking, blue eyes. Maybe you *should* get a tattoo. Maybe I should too. Maybe we can pick out something together."

I sniffed. "That would be nice, Talon. But I know you're not really into tattoos."

"I'm into you, blue eyes. Tattoos are important to you, and I can't let what happened to me rule my life. Getting a tattoo might be a good way of showing myself that it doesn't."

"Let's not rush into anything, okay?" I said. "We have all the time in the world. It doesn't matter whether we get a tattoo tomorrow or ten years from now or never. What matters is that you are here, and you're healing, and I'm here, and I love you, and I want to be with you more than anything in the whole world."

Then Talon turned to me, his gaze meeting mine, his eyes dark and burning, tears brimming.

I could see he was trying to choke them back. I touched his face, skimming one away. "It's okay, Talon. Everything is going to be okay."

And then this man—this strong, beautiful, amazing man who'd had his innocence ripped from him at such a tender age yet was a hero to so many—cried in my arms.

★ ★ ★ ★

Later, I lay awake in my own room at the ranch house. I desperately wanted to sleep next to Talon in his bed, but I didn't ask. He wasn't ready for that yet, and though I knew in my heart and soul that he would never harm me, he wasn't sure. And I wasn't about to push him.

My heart was still breaking. I couldn't even imagine what had truly gone on. I knew he'd glossed over a lot of it for my sake. I had wanted to tell him that he didn't need to, that I could take it, but I had been determined not to interrupt him, to let him say what he needed to say, the way he needed to say it.

Eventually I must've fallen asleep, because the next thing

I knew, I opened my eyes and light was streaming in through the window. I woke up and hopped in the shower, washing my hair and body. After toweling off, I sneaked into Marj's room and grabbed a robe again. She was still in the city because she had cooking class today.

I went to the kitchen, started a pot of coffee, and then crept silently down the hallway to the other end of the house to Talon's room. I opened the door slowly and quietly. I walked to the sitting area and into the bedroom. He was asleep on his back, his arms strewn over his forehead in his custom sleeping position. Roger lay at his feet, his head bobbing up at my entrance.

"Hey there, boy," I whispered.

Roger panted.

I didn't want to wake Talon. He was no doubt emotionally spent. So I decided to creep back out.

"Come on, boy," I said to Roger. "You need to go out?"

The little dog hopped up off the bed and followed me. As I walked out of the bedroom and the sitting room, I heard a voice.

"Blue eyes?"

I turned back in. Talon's dark eyes were open.

"I'm so sorry. I didn't mean to wake you. I just thought the dog might need to go out."

"Okay. Yeah, let him out. And then come back in here. I want to hold you."

I smiled. Sounded good to me. I let Roger out the back and then filled up a bowl of water for him and set it on the deck. Then I went back to Talon.

"You're wearing too many clothes," he said groggily.

"This is just an old robe of Marj's. I don't have any more

clothes here, remember? And I didn't want to put on that green dress from last night."

"You look smoking hot in that dress."

My cheeks warmed. "I'm glad you like it."

"I like you better out of it."

This time my body warmed.

"Come and sit with me."

I approached the bed and sat down. He took my hand.

"Did I do the right thing?" he asked. "Telling you?"

I nodded. "It's best that I know. I know it was hard for you, and it was hard for me to hear it. But now I understand you so much better. I love you, Talon. I want to understand you."

"You're sure none of it turned you off?"

"Oh my God, why would it? None of this was your fault. If the same thing had happened to me, would you feel any differently about me?"

He shook his head. "No. Of course not. But it's different when it happens to a boy."

"The only thing that's different is that it's less common. That doesn't mean it's not just as traumatic for a boy—in fact, it's probably more so."

"I sure wouldn't wish it on anyone, living or dead. Except maybe the three fuckers who did it to me."

"I can't say I blame you for that." I rubbed his hand. "And maybe we will find them. But Talon, just because Nico Kostas has a tattoo just like the one you remember and Larry Wade is missing a toe doesn't mean you found two of the perpetrators."

His body tensed and he went rigid. Shit. I shouldn't have said that.

"But we don't need to talk about that right now," I said, hoping to defuse the situation. "Would you like some breakfast? I can make scrambled eggs. And toast. That's about it."

"I don't feel like eating right now, blue eyes."

I must've looked concerned, because he said, "I'm all right. Just tired. Let me sleep for a few more hours, okay?"

I caressed his cheek. "I'd like to snuggle up beside you."

"I know, baby. One day, I promise."

I leaned down and brushed my lips over his. "I love you, Talon."

"I love you too, blue eyes."

I left the room and quietly closed the door. I went back to the kitchen, let Roger in, and prepared him some breakfast of kibble with a raw egg on top. I poured myself a cup of coffee and then made myself a piece of toast and some scrambled eggs. Once I sat down, though, I found I wasn't very hungry after all. I took one bite of the toast and picked at the eggs. I did drink a whole cup of coffee and then filled another.

Would Wendy Madigan mind if I called her on Saturday morning? She seemed to genuinely care about the Steels, and she had told me to come back to her once Talon told me everything. At the time, I'd had no idea what everything was, but I sure did now, and I had many questions.

I took my dishes to the sink, refilled my coffee once more, and headed to my room. My cell phone was charging on the nightstand. It was ten o'clock, certainly not early by anyone's standards. What the hell? I was on pins and needles to know what else she could tell me.

My pulse racing, I punched in her number.

"Hello, Jade," she said into my ear.

"Hi, Wendy. I hope it's not a problem to call you on a Saturday."

She sighed. "No, I've been expecting your call. And I'm not surprised it's during off hours."

I wasn't sure what she meant by that, but I didn't want to pry. I had a lot of other prying to do. "I had a long talk with Talon last night. He told me everything."

"By everything, what exactly do you mean?"

Did she really expect me to spell it out for her? It had been so hard hearing it from Talon's lips, and I wasn't sure I could say it. "Wendy..."

"I need to know, Jade, before I can tell you anything else."

"All right." I sighed. "He told me about what happened to him when he was ten. That he was abducted by two masked men and held captive for almost two months by three men. He told me what they did to him." I fought the nausea that crept up my throat. "And he told me of his eventual escape."

"I see." Silence for what seemed like hours but was probably only a couple of minutes.

"Wendy?"

"I'm here. I haven't talked about these things in...well... twenty-five years."

"Talon is in therapy, Wendy. He's healing, but I think it would really help him to heal if he knew who these perpetrators were. So that they could be brought to justice. Do you know who they are?"

"Not all of them."

God. My heart stampeded in my chest. That meant she knew at least one of them. And she could tell me. I could tell Talon. We could find him. We could lock him up for good.

"Oh my God. Who were they?"

"Before I tell you any more," she said, "there are some things you need to understand."

"I'm listening."

"You were right about Larry Wade and Daphne Steel. They were half-brother and half-sister. Larry is Daphne's elder by five years. They didn't grow up together. Larry stayed with his mother. But they did know each other."

"Why did the Steels try to cover up that relationship? Why would anyone care?"

"Because Larry was sick. And he was one of the three men who held Talon captive."

My heart nearly stopped, and my bowels churned. Sickness oozed within me. I had always known he was backward, unethical, but this...

My God. Talon was right.

"Jade?"

I cleared my throat. "Yeah. I'm okay."

"I'm sure this is a shock."

"No, not as much as it could be. Talon had already decided that he was one of them. I guess it'll be good for me to tell him that he's right."

"Jade—"

"What I don't understand, Wendy, is why didn't they have him arrested twenty-five years ago? He should be in prison."

"It's a long story. I can give you the short version now. We'll need to meet in person, maybe even with Talon, for me to tell you everything."

"Oh, no. I want you to tell me everything now. You promised."

"I will tell you everything. Right now I can only tell you the gist. I made a promise a long time ago never to reveal any of this except to Talon himself when the time was right."

"What the fuck does that mean? When the time was right?

This poor man has been through hell. He's been carrying this around for twenty-five years and is only just now getting the help he needs."

"Talon had to decide for himself when to get help."

"That is such bullshit! Someone should have helped him. His fucking parents should've helped him."

"Calm down, Jade. I can't say that I disagree with you. As much as I loved Brad, I didn't agree with everything he did. But he felt he had his reasons. Number one was his clinically insane wife."

"What? Are you saying Talon's mom was certifiably nuts?"

"She was never diagnosed with anything, but based on my dealings with her, I'd say she probably had both bipolar disorder and borderline personality disorder. Either that or narcissistic personality disorder."

I didn't know much about psychology, but I knew that double diagnosis meant trouble. "Why didn't the woman get help? Maybe she wouldn't have taken her own life."

"Brad tried. She refused. She was a very troubled woman, Jade. But she did dote on those boys. I truly do think that she loved them. The girl though—I don't think she ever really bonded with her. After all, she killed herself when Marjorie was barely two."

"Maybe she had convinced herself that Marjorie wasn't going to live after she was born so early. And then couldn't deal with it when she did." I was just tossing out words. I had no idea what I was saying.

"You may well be right," Wendy said. "I really have no idea, and I can't speculate. Daphne Steel was... Well, I'll just say it. She was a mess."

"All right, but none of this tells me why they didn't turn Larry in to the police."

"Part of it was the fact that he was Daphne's brother. Her father begged her not to turn Larry in. Her father said that Larry was sick, that he needed help, and that prison would kill him. Still, Brad would have none of it, but Daphne... She wasn't close to Larry. Like I said, they hadn't grown up together. But she *was* close to her father. If ever there had been a daddy's girl, it was Daphne Steel. So she thought about it. But in the end, she agreed with Brad that Larry had to be arrested."

"Then why wasn't he?"

"A day later, before he could be arrested, Larry ended up in the hospital. He had been severely beaten, most likely by the two other men who'd abducted Talon. Larry ended up nearly dying from the beating, but he never would name who they were."

"Why on earth would they have beaten him?"

"Because, Jade, Larry is the one who helped Talon escape."

CHAPTER THIRTY

Talon

The dreams came again. I was back, walking on the outskirts of the Walkers' small ranch, but it wasn't Ryan with me, clutching at my hand. No. It was Jade. Jade, who looked up at me with innocent steely blue eyes, who trusted me to protect her.

But when the masked men came, and when they grabbed her, I wasn't able to stop them. They dragged her away, all the while she was screaming, "Talon, help me! Help me! Help me!" Until she disappeared into the rundown shack.

I ran toward the shack, but my feet were stuck in mud. I was sinking in quicksand, and all around me, disembodied arms and legs came up from the mud to mock me.

"Help! Help!" I screamed. "I'm sinking! I'm sinking!"

In the abyss, a disembodied head floated upward, laughing at me.

"You couldn't help me, Talon. I died anyway. You didn't get here in time. And now you will die too."

I stared into the dead eyes of Luke Walker.

"No!"

And then my head went under.

I held my breath as long as I could, but soon I was forced to breathe in. Mud, dirt, slime entered my mouth, my nose...

The end...

The—

* * * *

I shot up in bed.

My heart was beating out of my chest. What the fuck? A new dream?

I had to talk to Dr. Carmichael. She had given me her number, but I had never used it, other than to call to make an appointment. She told me point blank that she didn't normally give out her cell number except in rare cases. I guessed I was one of those rare cases.

I had come so far. I had told Jade everything, and she hadn't turned away from me. I had to get through this. And I wasn't going to be able to get through it if I continued to have horrible and disgusting dreams. I looked at my cell phone. Ten thirty. Not too early to call.

I punched in Dr. Carmichael's number.

"This is Melanie."

"Hi. It's...Talon. Talon Steel."

"Yes, Talon, I recognized your number. Did you want to try to get an appointment today?"

"No. I mean, I was wondering if you could talk to me now."

"Of course. Are you all right?"

"Yeah. I mean no, but yeah. I'm not suicidal or anything. I'm not going to do anything stupid. But I'm a little freaked."

"Tell me what's going on."

"I told Jade everything last night."

"I see. And how did it go?"

"It was...hard. I mean, I knew it would be. But still it was hard."

"How did she take it?"

"She bawled. I bawled. But we got through it."

"And none of it mattered to her, did it?"

I sighed. "No."

"Is that what you need to talk to me about?"

"No. I just had a really freaky dream." As I told Dr. Carmichael about the dream, my skin chilled. "It's different than any other dream I've had. I really don't know why I would have it now, right after I told Jade."

"Well, Talon, you've always been able to protect everyone. Everyone except yourself. Now you finally have the person who means everything to you, so you're afraid that you won't be able to protect her."

"It can't be that simple."

"Dreams are never simple. But that's my initial thought. You can come into the office if you want, and I can take you through guided hypnosis. That might give us more valuable information."

"No, I don't want to do that. At least not today. I guess I was just surprised by it all. I mean, I woke up in a cold sweat."

"Understandable. But dreams are usually manifestation of fears, sometimes fears we don't even realize we have. And that's a very legitimate fear."

"But she trusts me, Doc. She fucking trusts me."

"Of course she does. With good reason. You're a very trustworthy person."

"But what if I can't protect her?"

"There are no guarantees in life, Talon. I only wish that there were. But you will protect her. You protected her from her ex, remember? Even though he wasn't a threat. And if there was a legitimate threat to her, you would do everything within your power to protect her. Your feet would not get caught in quicksand. It was just a dream."

I suddenly felt very foolish. "Will the dreams ever stop?"

"They may never stop completely. But I feel certain that they will lessen. And you'll find, in time, that they don't bother you nearly as much. Even this time, I've talked you down in a matter of minutes. That wouldn't have happened three months ago."

I couldn't disagree with her. "All right. I think I'm okay now. Thanks for talking to me, Doc."

"I'll always be here for you, Talon. For as long as you need me."

And I knew she would be.

Just like Jade would be.

As I said goodbye and hung up, Jade came running into my bedroom, Roger at her heels.

"Talon, thank God you're awake. You need to get up."

"What's going on, blue eyes?"

"I just got off the phone with Wendy Madigan."

Wendy Madigan? That was a blast from the past. How did Jade know about her? "Wendy?"

"Yeah."

"But how?"

"I found her name at the bottom of that local news article about your heroics when you came back from overseas."

Okay. But that didn't help me understand why Jade was on the phone with her.

"I'll explain all this later, but right now we need to act quickly. You were right, Talon. Larry Wade was one of the three men who abducted you."

CHAPTER THIRTY-ONE

Jade

His eyes widened into circles. He said nothing. In fact, he looked almost catatonic for a few moments. When I got to the point where I was actually beginning to worry, he finally blinked.

"What?"

I sat down next to him on the bed and took his trembling hand. "I've been talking to Wendy for a while. After I found her name on the article about you, I figured she had some information, and she confirmed that she did. Today she decided to give it to me."

He gulped. "Why today?"

"She felt an obligation toward you and your family. She didn't want to divulge anything until you had told me everything."

"She told you that something happened to me?"

I nodded. "But Talon, don't be angry with her. You told me yourself that something had happened to you, remember?"

Talon stared straight ahead, not speaking.

"Talon? Do you understand what this means? We can have him arrested. One of your abductors will see justice served."

He shook his head, blinking as if to clear his head. "We don't know where he is."

"Wendy told me he owns some land in Montana. We'll start there. But honestly, he'd be stupid to go there."

"And if that turns up nothing?"

"We put the cops on it. We hire the best PIs in the business. For once, aren't you glad that money is no object?"

Again, silence.

What was up with him?

"Baby, this is good news. Once we find Larry, we can force him to tell us who the other two are. Let's get on it. Let's get Jonah and Ryan and Marj, and we'll get started. Not only do you have the money to bankroll a full-scale investigation, but the woman you love happens to be the city attorney of Snow Creek right now. I have access to all the databases. We'll find him, Talon. I know we'll find him."

Still he stared straight ahead.

"What's wrong? I don't get it."

He shook his head slowly, methodically. "I just don't believe it. I mean, I wanted to believe that I had identified two of my abductors, but inside, inside my objective brain, I knew it was unlikely." He turned to me, his eyes unreadable. "Is there really an end to this in sight?"

I took his hand, massaging my thumb into his palm. "Nothing can erase what you went through, but we can at least find one of them and bring him to justice."

And again, silence.

"You should be ecstatic. What's wrong?"

Silence again.

Then, "It's just..." He raked his hands through his tousled bedhead. "I'm not sure how to say this. How to make you understand."

I continued to rub his palm with my thumb, aching

to comfort him. I had no idea what could be the matter, but he needed to know I was here for him. That I wasn't going anywhere. Ever.

"You can tell me anything. You know I'll understand."

He drew in a deep breath. "All these years I've lived with this horror, and until recently, I never even thought about trying to heal. And now, with you, I finally found a reason to go on. And through you I found other reasons, my brothers and sister, my ranch, even myself. And I'm beginning. I'm moving forward."

"Yes, you're doing great. So what's the matter?"

"I'm not sure. I'm not sure I can put it into words. But if we find one of them, finally put one phase of this to rest...it's gone. That part of my life is finally gone."

"And that's a bad thing?"

He shook his head. "I told you that you wouldn't understand."

"Try me. Talk to me, Talon."

"It was horrible. No child—hell, no living being—should go through what I went through. But I did go through it. It was my own. It was horrible, heinous, awful. But it was *mine*."

I squeezed his hand. I wanted to take him into my arms and comfort him, but I wasn't sure that was what he needed right now. "Why do you want to hold on to this, Talon?"

"I don't. At least I think I don't. I told you it was hard to explain. But it's been part of me for so long."

"It will always be a part of you. It will always be part of what made you the man you are today. And I think you're an incredible man."

"I'm trying, blue eyes. I'm really trying."

"I know you are. You've had to own this. You've had to

walk this path alone for so long. But you're not alone anymore, Talon. I'm here for you. Your brothers are here for you. Marjorie is here for you. The six people you saved that day in Iraq—they're all here for you. The hundreds of employees on this ranch who depend on you for their livelihood—they're all here for you. You have a lot of people in your corner, a lot of people who would do anything for you."

"Could it really—I mean really—be over? Really over?"

My sweet, wonderful Talon. He'd lived so long with this burden. "It was over twenty-five years ago, baby. You've been free since then. You just didn't know it. It's time we took matters into our own hands, time we brought those perpetrators to justice. And now we can. So, my love, it's time."

He turned to me, his eyes misted over, and nodded. "Time to let it go."

★ ★ ★ ★

As expected, Larry wasn't in Montana, but with the Steels' money and a private investigation team, along with help from the local police force and state patrol, Larry was picked up three days later in southern New Mexico. He'd been using an alias and had been working at a hatch chile farm, trying to make enough money to cross the border.

And in his personals? Colin's wallet and phone.

That sicko had been the one who called me using Colin's phone.

He'd been brought back to Grand Junction and was being held in the county jail for now. I sat, at the visitors' window, waiting for him. I'd told Talon I was going, and I'd offered to take him with me, but he had chosen not to come. Probably just as well. I wasn't sure he could have held it together. I'd had to nearly tie him down—along with Jonah and Ryan—to keep him from going after Larry himself.

I didn't know what I was going to say to Larry. What could one say to such a sick person? He most likely had killed Colin, too, though with no body, a murder would be difficult to prove. There would be no reasoning with Larry. A psychopath couldn't be reasoned with. Still, I had to try. The prosecuting attorney had offered him a deal if he named the two others. I was here to convince him to take it.

His hands and feet were cuffed when a guard let him in. He was dressed all in orange, the little hair he had in disarray and his countenance fatigued. He sat down and picked up the telephone.

"Jade," he said. "Are you here to represent me?"

My eyes must've nearly popped out of my head. Had I heard him right? "I'm the acting city attorney now, Larry. Even if I wanted to, I couldn't represent you. I'm not sure the mayor would look too kindly upon me moonlighting to represent my former boss who happens to be a child molester."

He sighed. "You'd be surprised what the mayor is capable of."

"It shouldn't surprise me what *you've* turned out to be capable of, Larry. I mean, with your questionable ethics and all. Still, I never would've thought you to be such a sick criminal."

"That's because I'm not a sick criminal, Jade."

I laughed out loud. Couldn't help myself. "You do know that we have ample evidence against you."

"I had nothing to do with that other guy's disappearance. I don't know how his things got into my possession. As for the other stuff, I was coerced. I've told the police the whole story.

They're offering me a deal if I name the two others."

"First of all, you were not coerced. You're a sick pedophile, Larry. If you were truly coerced, you wouldn't have taken your turn with him like the other two did."

"I'm telling you, they forced me."

"They forced you to get a hard dick for a little boy? Sure." This conversation was rapidly coming to an end. "Look, I'm not here to argue the point. I know exactly what you did. Talon told me everything. What I'm here for is to ask you to take that deal. I want those other two brought to justice."

Larry shook his head. "I can't."

"Why not? You're going to prison no matter what. Are you afraid of them from prison?"

"I won't roll over on them. They would do the same for me."

"Really? You think they would? Didn't you just say you were coerced? And aren't they the ones who had you beaten to a pulp when you helped Talon escape?"

His eyes lit up. "You're right. I helped the boy escape. Don't I deserve some compassion for that?"

"Jesus Christ. This wasn't just some kid. It was heinous no matter what, but he was your nephew, for God's sake."

Larry's lips trembled. "He wasn't supposed to be there. When the other two brought him back, I begged them to let him go."

"So you weren't one of the ones who was at that little shack that day with Luke Walker?"

He shook his head. "No. Those were the other two. When they brought him back and I recognized him, I told them they had to let him go. That the Steels were important people."

"Larry," I said through gritted teeth, "tell me who they

fucking are."

"I can't. They'll kill me."

"Is one of them Nico Kostas?"

Larry gave me a poker face. I couldn't read him at all, and I was pretty good at reading people. He wasn't going to budge.

"This is a waste of time." I started to hang up the phone, but Larry held up his hand.

"Jade, wait."

I put the receiver back to my ear. "What do you want now?"

"They held him for a little less than two months. When it became clear that he was near death, I started giving him more food. I was the one in charge of feeding him. I was just a lackey, Jade. A lackey."

"A lackey who sexually abused a little boy. An innocent little boy. Your nephew."

"I regret it, Jade. I regret all of it."

"Is that supposed to mean something to me? To Talon? To his parents, may they rest in peace?"

"Brad and Daphne forgave me. They didn't turn me in. If they were willing to let me go—"

"Brad and Daphne are dead. Daphne took her own life because she couldn't live with what you had done to her son. She left her children without a mother. One of them doesn't remember her. Talon needed his mother, Larry. And because of you, he didn't have her."

"Would you please just let me explain?"

"How do you explain this? How do you explain your sick mind?"

"Talon was never supposed to be taken."

"And you think that makes this all right? What about the

other six kids?"

"I wasn't involved with any of those."

"You expect me to believe that? No one's going to believe that, Larry."

"Jade, I let Talon go. Talon is alive because of me."

"This conversation is over."

He stood again, urging me to wait with his hand. "Doesn't that mean anything to you? That he's alive because of me? They killed all the others. Cut them up like firewood. It was sick, I tell you. Sick."

"I know. Except for the one body that was found. I know what they did to the others because Talon told me. They made him watch as they carved up Luke Walker. They made a ten-year-old boy watch that sickness."

"I...I had nothing to do with that."

"Sorry. I don't buy it. You were just as much a part of this as they were. So do yourself a favor and name the other two."

He shook his head. "They'll kill me."

That was a great argument as far as I was concerned. If Larry ended up toes up, I didn't really care. "I've got to tell you, Larry. You're lucky to be locked up. If you were out, Talon and his brothers would make quick work of you."

"Steels. They think they own the place."

"Do you listen to yourself sometimes? You want them to grant you mercy, and you talk about them like that?"

"I'm...sorry. Just... He really is alive because of me, Jade. I drugged his food and let him sneak out. When he lost consciousness, and I put clothes on him and drove him to about half an hour away from his ranch at night. I knew when he woke up, someone would find him. And someone did. He's alive. He was allowed to grow up. Because of me."

"Because of you, Larry, he grew up never dealing with this. It was all brushed under the rug because you wouldn't name the others and because Brad and Daphne made the decision to let you go."

"They let me go because I saved their son. I had to leave the state."

The five million dollars. *Of course.* "They paid you, didn't they? They gave you a chunk of their millions to get you out of Colorado and away from their children."

"No, no, they didn't. They didn't give me anything. But yes, they did make me leave. Said they'd have me arrested if I didn't stay far away."

Liar. I'd have to push Wendy some more about that transfer. Of course they'd paid Larry. Where else could it have gone? "I don't believe you."

"I left. I didn't come back until after Brad died. I was broke, dead broke. My wife had left me. I needed a job, so the mayor appointed me city attorney. I was a good city attorney, Jade."

I couldn't even respond to that. The man was delusional.

"Please, Jade. Brad and Daphne chose to let me go."

"I don't think Talon is as forgiving as his parents were. And I can tell you right now I'm not. So unless you tell me who those other two were, I'm leaving and I will see you in court."

Larry rubbed his forehead. "I wish I could. I can't."

I hung up the phone, turned, and walked away.

CHAPTER THIRTY-TWO

Talon

"To moving forward." Jonah lifted his glass of red wine.

I sat at one of the tables out on our beautiful deck, surrounded by the four people I loved most in the world.

My older brother, always so steadfast and strong, always the first to take any blame and possessing such a fierce desire to protect the rest of us. That he hadn't been able to protect that day me haunted him still, even though I'd begged him to give up the guilt. To move on. Perhaps his toast meant that he would, finally, commit to letting go himself.

My younger brother, the one who'd followed me around when I was a kid, had been a royal pain in my ass but always wanted to slip his little hand in mine and go wherever I went. I was so thankful he had gotten away that day. And because I had protected him and told him to run, I was forever his hero. He would always have my back. But he needed to move on too, just like Joe and I did.

My baby sister, who in her own way had saved me. When I came home, she had just come home from the hospital. Everyone had thought she would die because she was so premature, but little Marjorie was strong. Strong as an ox. So beautiful and so innocent. A tiny porcelain doll who stole my heart as soon as I laid eyes on her. She was the only proof I had back then of any good left in the world. I would've done anything for her, and I still would.

And Jade. My beautiful Jade, whose mother was on the mend and with whom she was beginning to make peace. She'd been fighting her own demons, but still, she'd been here for me since she arrived in Snow Creek. I'd tried so hard to push her way at first, but I never had the strength to let her go. And even if I had, she would've come barreling back into my life. Because she wasn't going to let me go. It was through Jade that I had finally learned that I wanted to live. Not just to exist but to live—to embrace life, to hold on to another person. Life would never be easy for me, but with Jade, I would make it. If I started to drown, she would pull me out of the water.

And I would do the same for her.

She was my forever. And it felt so good to finally want a forever.

I raised my glass in tandem with the others. "To moving forward," we all said together.

Marjorie and Felicia had cooked a celebratory dinner of beef tenderloin with fresh Colorado peach salsa from our own orchard, broccoli rabe, mashed potatoes with garlic and cilantro, and wild mushroom ragout. The table was decorated with three vases of multicolored roses that Marj had brought in from the florist in town. My brothers and sister smiled. Jade sat next to me, squeezing my thigh every now and then when I got quiet, just letting me know that she was there.

That she would always be there.

We didn't talk about Larry Wade or the fact that he refused to roll over on the other two. We didn't talk about anything of import really. We just laughed together, cried a little bit together, and committed to moving on.

When it got quiet, I turned to Jade. "Blue eyes?"

"Yeah?"

"I want you to move back in here. Please."

She bit her lip.

"Oh, please, Jade, please," Marjorie echoed.

Her beautiful lips burst into that smile I had grown to love so much, that smile that could fix anything that was wrong with my day, with my life.

"All right. I'd love nothing more than to be back here. It's what I always wanted. But it wasn't the right time before now."

We all toasted again while Felicia served us peach cobbler, hot from the oven, topped with vanilla-bean ice cream.

There was a word for how I felt at that moment, a word I hadn't used in ages to describe anything about myself.

Happy.

★ ★ ★ ★

Later, I took my lovely Jade to bed and let her undress me.

"I want to take care of you tonight," she said.

I smiled. "Only if you do it while you're naked."

She let out an adorable giggle. "If those are your terms, I accept."

She undressed, more quickly than I wanted her to, but what did it matter, as long as she ended up naked?

"Lie down, baby. On your back. I'm going to worship that gorgeous body of yours." She smiled.

My cock was already hard for her. I could take her now and be ready for more in no time. "Come and sit on me first," I said. "I need to be inside you."

She shook her head, her eyes mischievous. "Oh, no, you

don't. You always get your way in bed. Tonight I'm getting mine."

My nerves jumped a little. I wasn't comfortable being submissive. She knew that. I grabbed her and pulled her on top of me for a passionate kiss, reminding her of who was in charge in this room.

The kiss left us both breathless, but she was not to be swayed.

"Please, Talon. Let me take care of you."

I could deny her nothing. Even though the situation made me uncomfortable, I relented.

"Relax," she said. "You know I would never harm you."

And when her soft lips caressed the sensitive skin of my neck, I untied my muscles and let go. She trailed kisses over my shoulder and then down my upper arm and lower arm to my hand, where she kissed each finger and then massaged my hand with her own. She kissed back up to my other arm, repeating her movements, until she stroked her sweet tongue over my chest, licking one of my nipples, which hardened under her touch. She sucked a bit at them, and my cock hardened even further.

She continued downward, kissing my abdomen, burying her nose in my bush and inhaling.

"God, you smell so good, Talon."

"Please, baby, suck my cock."

She lifted her head and met my gaze. "In good time." She smiled.

I was on edge, ready to go fucking crazy. I grabbed fistfuls of the comforter to keep from grabbing her, turning her over, and fucking her into oblivion.

She massaged my thighs with her hands and her lips down

to my calves, to my feet, my toes. And then back up again. She spread my legs and pushed my thighs forward.

I tensed.

"Shh," she said. "Let me."

She kissed the inside of my thighs, the crease between my thighs and ass, and then gave me tiny kisses on my balls, which were bunched up and ready to release at any moment.

Then, finally, she took my cock into her mouth, as slowly she trailed her finger down the crease of my ass.

Until she found that place.

I jerked.

"Shh," she said again. "Let me. Trust me."

I did trust her, but tension filled me.

She moved her lips from my cock and began to work it with her hand. She withdrew her other hand from the crease of my ass and wet it with her tongue. Slowly, that hand drifted down to where it had been.

Still tense. Still afraid.

But again her soft voice. "Take it back, Talon. Take your body back. It was never theirs. It's yours, and it's mine."

And she gently probed through the tight rim of muscle.

I gasped.

"Easy," she said. "Getting through that ring of muscle is the hardest part."

I'd said the same words to her.

Her voice soothed me as I eased the tension from my muscles. Determination surged through me, determination to do what she had asked. To take my body back. To give in to the pleasure.

"Let yourself go. Let this feel good," she said.

I lifted my neck, keeping my eyes open, so I could watch

her, to know that it was her.

Needed to know it was her.

She worked farther in, still pumping my cock with her other hand.

I was still hard, still wanted her so goddamned much.

And as I watched her, her steely blue eyes fixed upon me, her gentle hands working parts of my body, I began to relax.

I began to feel pleasure.

"That's it," she said. "It's me. Always me. No one but me. And I love you. I love you so much."

My breath caught, and I leaned back onto the pillow, closing my eyes.

Her mouth replaced her hand on my shaft, and she continued to probe my ass as she sucked me.

Oh my God. So fucking good.

When my balls bunched up and the tiny convulsions started, I groaned. "I'm going to come, baby. I want you to swallow all of me. Swallow me, baby. Make me yours."

And when I climaxed, and she lapped up all of my essence, I finally, *finally*...let go.

★ ★ ★ ★

We woke together the next morning, sunlight streaming in through my window, Roger nestled at her feet.

She looked up at me as I stroked her soft cheek.

"Okay?" she asked.

"Better than okay. This was the first night we slept all night together."

She smiled. "And nothing bad happened."

I pressed my lips lightly against hers. "From now on, we

sleep together, in my bed—our bed—every night."

"I'd love nothing more." She closed her eyes and let out a sigh.

One of the bouquets of roses that Marj had brought home from town yesterday sat on my night table. I grabbed a red one, and slowly I trailed the soft petals across her cheeks, her lips.

"Mmm"—Jade opened her eyes—"that feels nice. I love roses. Even when you threw me out of the house that night, I knew I'd be back someday. I knew you felt something for me. Because of the rose you left on my pillow."

I jerked, dropping the rose onto the bed next to Jade. My pulse raced. "What?"

She sat up. "What's wrong?"

"What are you talking about, blue eyes?"

"The next morning, after you asked me to leave the house. You left a rose on my pillow."

I swallowed, my heart thundering. "Baby, I love you. But I didn't leave a rose on your bed that morning."

EPILOGUE

Jonah

I hadn't seen Bryce Simpson in a couple of years, so when I got a phone call, I was surprised. He'd run off to Las Vegas and married some woman he'd only known a couple of weeks. He was my age, thirty-eight, and like me had been a bachelor most of his life. Now he was coming home to Snow Creek to visit his parents—the mayor and his wife. Not only that, but he had a new baby boy, nine months old.

I was sitting in Rita's café, drinking a cup of coffee, when he came in to meet me, toting his new son.

I stood. "Bryce, man, so good to see you." I gave him a man-hug. "Quite a little guy you've got there."

The little boy was adorable, with light-blond hair and blue eyes. Bryce's blond hair had turned a silvery gray.

"So where's the missus?"

"We split up."

"Oh? I'm sorry to hear that." Though I was not surprised. I'd always thought Bryce more level-headed than to run off to Vegas with somebody he didn't know very well.

"Yeah, it was a mistake. But I got Henry here out of it. She didn't want custody. In fact, she hardly ever requests visitation."

"Doing the single-dad thing?"

"It was never my plan. In fact, I never thought I'd have kids. But now that this little guy is here, I don't know how I ever got along without him. You ever think of settling down?"

A loaded question if ever there was one. For the longest time, I had never wanted to saddle anyone with my life, as filled with guilt as it was. But now my brother Talon was moving on after twenty-five years from the abduction that had occurred when he was ten, the event that had affected both me and our younger brother, Ryan, as well.

Talon had a girl now, and they'd probably be tying the knot soon. If he could move forward, have a relationship, have a family, maybe it was time I did too. As I looked at Bryce and his little son, I felt a yearning that was new to me.

"Honestly, I haven't. Not for a long time anyway. But you never know. Maybe I'll meet a nice woman who wants an old rancher like me."

"A rancher who's richer than God? I'd say there are a lot of them out there." Bryce let out a laugh.

I didn't want someone who was after my money. Enough of them had come around during my life. But if I could find something like what Talon had with Jade, I sure wouldn't turn my back on it.

"Do you think he'd let me hold him?" I asked Bryce, nodding to Henry.

"Sure. He's a really good-natured little guy." He handed the baby to me.

Henry gurgled, and I set him on the table facing me, holding on to him so he wouldn't fall. He gave me a big toothless grin. He was a healthy-looking boy, looked a lot like his dad. As I held his little hands, I noticed a birthmark on his arm.

"I don't remember you having a birthmark. Did he get

that from his mom?"

Bryce shook his head. "Probably from my dad. He has a dark one just like that. Shaped kind of like the state of Texas."

Continue the Steel Brothers Saga with Jonah's story in

Melt

Coming December 20th, 2016

MESSAGE FROM HELEN HARDT

Dear Reader,

Thank you for reading *Possession*. If you want to find out about my current backlist and future releases, please like my Facebook page: **www.facebook.com/HelenHardt** and join my mailing list: **www.helenhardt.com/signup/**. I often do giveaways. If you're a fan and would like to join my street team to help spread the word about my books, you can do so here: **www.facebook.com/groups/hardtandsoul/**. I regularly do awesome giveaways for my street team members.

If you enjoyed the story, please take the time to leave a review on a site like Amazon or Goodreads. I welcome all feedback.

I wish you all the best!

Helen

ACKNOWLEDGMENTS

I made myself cry several times while writing *Possession*. Actually, this whole series so far has made me cry. I hope very much that you've all enjoyed this final volume of Jade and Talon's journey. Bringing Talon to the point where he could finally let go has been both heart-wrenching and rewarding. And don't worry! We'll be seeing more of him and Jade.

Thanks so much to my amazing editors, Celina Summers and Michele Hamner Moore. Your guidance and suggestions were invaluable. Thank you to my line editor, Jenny Rarden, and my proofreaders, Angela Kelly and Claire Allmendinger. Thank you to all the great people at Waterhouse Press— Meredith, David, Kurt, Shayla, Jon, and Yvonne. The cover art for this series is beyond perfect, thanks to Meredith and Yvonne.

Thank you to the members of my street team, Hardt and Soul. HS members got the first look at *Possession*, and I appreciate all your support, reviews, and general good vibes. You ladies are the best!

Thanks to my always supportive family and friends and to all of the fans who eagerly waited for *Possession*. I hope you love it.

Be on the lookout for Jonah's story, beginning with *Melt*, out on December 20th, 2016!

ALSO BY HELEN HARDT

The Sex and the Season Series:
Lily and the Duke
Rose in Bloom
Lady Alexandra's Lover
Sophie's Voice
The Perils of Patricia (coming soon)

The Temptation Saga:
Tempting Dusty
Teasing Annie
Taking Catie
Taming Angelina
Treasuring Amber
Trusting Sydney
Tantalizing Maria (Coming October 25th, 2016)

Daughters of the Prairie:
The Outlaw's Angel
Lessons of the Heart
Song of the Raven

The Steel Brothers Saga:
Craving
Obsession
Possession
Melt (Coming December 20th, 2016)

DISCUSSION QUESTIONS

1. The theme of a story is its central idea or ideas. To put it simply, it's what the story *means*. How would you characterize the theme of *Possession?*

2. Discuss the author's use of flashbacks in *Possession*. How does it differ from the previous two books?

3. Have we learned anything new about Talon's past? Discuss how this does or does not make his character more understandable and sympathetic.

4. Discuss the character of Larry Wade. What might his childhood have been like? His relationship with his father? With Daphne? What was his role in Talon's abduction? Do you feel he is any less guilty than the others? Why or why not? Do you believe he had anything to do with Colin's disappearance?

5. Jonah and Ryan still can't admit that they're glad they weren't abducted. What does this say about them?

6. We learn more about Jade's mother, Brooke, in this book. Discuss her character. Do you think she will grow as a result of her life-threatening accident? Will she and Jade make peace?

7. Do you think Nico Kostas tampered the airbag in his car? Why or why not?

8. Where do you think the five million dollars went?

9. Discuss Talon's parents' decision to let Larry go. Do you agree? Why or why not?

10. Who do you think left the red rose on Jade's pillow in

Craving?

11. How does the relationship between Jade and Talon differ inside and outside the bedroom? Is Talon an alpha male or a beta male?

12. Where do you think Nico Kostas is, and how will he return? Did the revelation of the third kidnapper surprise you? Why or why not?

13. This is the end of Talon and Jade's trilogy, but their story is far from over. What might the future hold for them? Will Talon continue in therapy?

14. In the next story, *Melt,* Jonah becomes the hero. What might the future hold for him? Who might his heroine be?

ABOUT THE AUTHOR

New York Times and *USA Today* Bestselling author Helen Hardt's passion for the written word began with the books her mother read to her at bedtime. She wrote her first story at age six and hasn't stopped since. In addition to being an award winning author of contemporary and historical romance and erotica, she's a mother, a black belt in Taekwondo, a grammar geek, an appreciator of fine red wine, and a lover of Ben and Jerry's ice cream. She writes from her home in Colorado, where she lives with her family. Helen loves to hear from readers.

Visit her here:
www.facebook.com/HelenHardt

Jonah Steel is intelligent, rich, and hard-working. As the oldest of his siblings, he was charged by his father to protect them.

He failed in the worst way.

Dr. Melanie Carmichael has her own baggage. Although the renowned therapist was able to help Jonah's brother, she is struggling with feelings of inadequacy. When the oldest Steel walks into her office seeking solace, she can't turn her back.

As Melanie and Jonah attempt to work through their issues together, desperately trying to ignore the desire brewing between them, ghosts from both their pasts surface...and danger draws near.

Coming December 20th 2016!

726459